THE MARKET

J. M. STEELE

HYPERION · NEW YORK

First Edition
10 9 8 7 6 5 4 3 2 1
Designed by Elizabeth H. Clark
Printed in the United States of America
This book is set in Garamond 3.
Library of Congress Cataloging-in-Publication Data on file.
ISBN-13: 978-1-4231-0013-3
ISBN-10: 1-4231-0013-1
Reinforced binding
Visit www.hyperionbooksforchildren.com

BOOK ONE

·······

AN INITIAL PUBLIC OFFERING

CHAPTER

1

SOMEWHERE IN THE DISTANCE I heard a cell phone ringing, and I slipped in unnoticed through the side door. Gretchen's kitchen was crammed shoulder-to-shoulder with kids from Millbank, and the smell of sweat hung in the air. By the window a pony keg filled the sink, the tap hose snaking up into some meathead's slurping mouth. As two of his friends lifted him upside down for a keg stand, I pushed my way toward the living room, which—if possible—appeared even more packed. Everybody was dancing to pounding hip-hop, and the room was vibrating; shaking, in fact. As I took another step, I felt heat and sweat rise up like a wall in front of me.

I'm so out of my league.

Was I a social pariah at Millbank High School? No. But

I wasn't the "I" or the "T" of the It Crowd, either. For four long and safe years, I had been comfortable moving with the herd of the forgettable, but standing in the midst of this truly unforgettable party made me realize how lame my life at Millbank High School had been. Gretchen Tanner was *that* popular girl with the rich dad who gave her everything she wanted: a brand new Mercedes convertible, an AMEX black card so she could shop till she literally dropped, and unchaperoned parties on the weekends when her parents went out of town. Oh, and she was gorgeous. She basically lived a fairy-tale life. To those mere mortals—like yours truly—it was enough to make you want to barf. Yes, Gretchen and I were from two different worlds. The fact that over the past four years we'd said maybe two words to each other only made the invitation that I'd discovered stuck in the grille of my locker all the more baffling. No one else I knew had been invited to Gretchen's party. Not Dev. Not Callie.

So why me?

Already regretting the pink sweater set from Ann Taylor that my mother had talked me into wearing, I grabbed a Diet Coke from a cooler and positioned myself by the door to the patio. The party was divided into what I liked to call the Three Rings of Popularity, and I was definitely the only person from the third ring—i.e., the outer reaches of this particular social galaxy. Camped out in the living room were the solid members of the second ring, which was comprised tonight of Mike Talbot and the rest of the zero-and-fourteen soccer players who thought they had the world by the balls, the field hockey girls who were never cute enough to be super cool but had amazing bodies and liked to party, and a group of annoying sophomore cheerleaders still in uniform popping out yet another version of some lame-ass line dance, like the lemmings they were. Out on the patio, securely forming the first ring, was Gretchen's inner circle, aka The Proud Crowd: Jodi Letz, Elisa Estrada, and Carrie Bell. Their silver "P"s (the Proud Crowd's trademark emblem) glittered on chains around their necks, while JV wannabes mooned around them, hoping to gain access to this rarified world. Gretchen Tanner, the epicenter, the force around which everyone at Millbank High orbited, was nowhere in sight.

After a few minutes of wall-flowering, silently wondering how long I needed to stay before I could make a face-saving exit via the back door, I noticed Will Bochnowski walk in with Jack Clayton following close behind. If Gretchen had a male counterpart at Millbank High, it was Will B. I'd had a major crush on him for, like, two years— and let's be honest, *every* girl had a crush on Will B.— because, don't let the name fool you, he was a hottie of the highest order. Shaggy brown hair that hung down almost to his shoulders, eyes so blue that you could swim in them, and a body that was to die for; he was, in a word, *it*. Will was on his way to Vassar next year, and he fronted a band called Jane Austen's Secret Lover, which—rumor had it—had just signed a deal with an indie record label.

Jack Clayton, who I'd never actually seen without Will B., was the guitarist in the band and widely regarded as Will's sidekick (or his "Boy Wonder," as some less charitable people put it). Dressed conservatively—new jeans, a perfectly ironed dress shirt, and a baseball hat pulled low—he hardly cut the same figure as Will and pretty much traipsed in his shadow. As they passed by, neither one of them noticed me, and I found myself staring into the crowd blankly.

So how does a girl busy herself for an hour when she has no one to talk to at a party? Well . . .

She makes no fewer than three trips to the bathroom, where she leans against the sink and waits until someone knocks.

She studies the tomes on the bookshelves with an intensity bordering on religious.

She keeps moving and makes at least three "laps" around the house, wearing a perplexed expression that suggests she's searching for someone specific who just *has* to be in the next room.

She steps outside for an important call on her cell—at which point others in the vicinity may overhear phrases such as, *Oh my God!* or *Shut up!* or *That's soooo awesome!*

In short, she does anything not to look like a complete and total LOSER.

But after my fourth trip to the bathroom (the max, lest someone thinks you have some sort of problem—bladder, drug, or otherwise) and more than a handful of sideways glances cast my direction courtesy of the Proud Crowd, I decided I had to mix it up. Dying of thirst anyway, I wandered out to the pool, where another keg sat in a plastic garbage can. Despite the fact that I usually walked the straight-and-narrow path, I decided I needed a drink. In fact, I reasoned, I *deserved* a drink. Besides, I wasn't driving. My car was getting inspected, so, much to my chagrin, my mother had ferried me to Gretchen's house and I was supposed to call her when I was ready to leave.

I grabbed a plastic cup from the table and picked up the hose, but when I pressed the button on the nozzle, nothing came out. I tried shaking the keg to see if it was empty, but its weight revealed that it was very much still full. I tried the button again, and nothing but foam spurted out.

"Let me help you with that," I heard a voice say.

I looked up just in time to see Will Bochnowski approach.

My knees—no joke—buckled.

"You have to pump it first," he explained, and he grabbed the knob on top of the tap and lifted it.

"Oh, right," I mumbled, feeling like the biggest moron ever. "Of course."

He must have been dancing because in the cool night air, steam rose off his sweat-drenched head. He filled two cups—one for each of us—and leaned against a pillar.

"Kate Winthrop," he said.

"Yup, that's me."

That's me? I couldn't think of anything less retarded to say? What about "the one and only"? Or "in the flesh"? Or "the girl you've always wanted to date"?

"So how's it going?"

"Oh, you know," I replied. "Just doing my thing."

I noticed then that his eyes were a little glassy—like maybe he'd had too much to drink—and his head lolled a little to the side. It was sexy, whatever it was, and he exuded a level of confidence that was paralyzing. Maybe that explained why I seemed to have lost the power of speech.

"Good times, huh?" he said.

For the love of God, I just couldn't respond. I stood there starry-eyed, just watching his mouth open and shut. Finally I blurted out, "Uh-huh."

"Sounds like it."

"It's true," I laughed.

I can't believe I'm talking to Will B.

"This isn't your scene," he observed, and I felt my spirits dip. It was a sobering reminder. No, I wasn't of this world.

I said nothing.

"That's a good thing," he said, looking around with distaste in his eye.

From within the screened patio, Jack Clayton shouted out to Will. When I turned, I saw that Jack was staring directly at me—in a sort of weird way—like my talking to Will had irked him somehow.

"Let's go, B.!" Jack shouted again.

"Comin'!" Will yelled back.

I noticed then that there was a girl lurking behind Jack, peering out at us as well. Was it Gretchen? Or just one of her groupies? It was impossible to tell through the screen door.

Will drained his beer and tossed the cup in the garbage. "Well, that's my ride. Shine on, little sister."

I nodded and gave him a little smile (I think the fly on the wall would have said it was my pathetic attempt at flirting). Just as he passed me, he stopped and turned. He was close enough that I could smell his cologne—piney and masculine.

"You know, Kate," he said, "you were always the one I couldn't see."

I just stared back at him. I couldn't speak. After a beat, he shrugged his shoulders like he didn't have time to wait for somebody as slow-witted as me and then turned and walked away into the crowd.

What the hell did that mean?

It wasn't long after my talk with Will that I realized it was officially time to leave.

I'd nursed about a third of my lukewarm beer and wandered around the front of the house when I noticed that quiet music had replaced the heavy dance beats. The party was evolving into one of those intimate, core-group-only moments, and I suddenly felt alone. I had to leave. But how? My house was a good thirty minutes away, and I surely didn't have money to call a cab. Needless to say, if I wanted to leave this party with a minuscule sense of coolness, the good-ol' mom taxi service was out of the question.

I was standing on the front lawn, lamely staring out at Manhattan in the distance, when I heard the front door unlatch behind me. If there were part of me that was hoping to see Will standing there, offering to give me a ride home, it was quickly crushed. It wasn't Will.

It was Gretchen Tanner.

With a wiggle of her fingers that passed for a wave, she closed the door behind her and sauntered over to where I stood.

"Cute outfit," she remarked, gesturing toward my sweater set, and I felt myself go red. She could deliver a backhanded compliment better than Maria Sharapova. I knew how I looked: like a soccer mom.

Whatever you thought of Gretchen Tanner—she wielded her Queen Bee status like a mace—you had to hand it to her.

Even at the very end of the night, when the average girl looked a little worn-out and worse for wear, Gretchen was still a veritable vision of beauty. Dressed in a slinky white shift that must have cost a gajillion dollars, with a huge strand of what-I-could-only-presume-to-be real pearls wrapped casually around her wrist, she looked ridiculously beautiful. Next to her I felt like a cow . . . a tall, pink cow. I wondered in that split second what it must be like to be that rich, that beautiful, and that popular.

"So how's it going, Kate?"

"Great. Awesome party."

"Yeah," she said, looking bored. "It was okay."

I shifted my weight and watched her. For some reason Gretchen had always intimidated me, and the fact that she intimidated me annoyed me. Still, I summoned all my social decorum.

"Thanks so much for having me."

"Sorry?" Her head cocked to the side, and she squinted.

"You know, for inviting me."

"What made you think you were invited?"

"Um, um," I stammered. "Didn't you put an invitation in my—"

"Invitation?" She laughed as she cut me off. "Does this look like a party for sixth graders?"

I studied the ground, too humiliated to look her in the eye.

"But you wouldn't know, I guess," she continued. "No worries, Katie. Somebody must've played a little joke on you. Or me. I just hope it wasn't too boring for you."

"It was fine," I said, wanting at this point to evaporate into the ether. "I had a nice chat with Will."

As soon as his name came out of my mouth, Gretchen's face changed, tightening up like a sixty-year-old on her third face lift.

"Will likes to slum, Seventy-one."

I blinked.

"Seventy-one?"

"Forget it," she said, all her poise returning.

Behind her, the front door opened again, and out stepped Gretchen's number-one protégée, Jodi Letz. Spotting me, she exhaled, looking exasperated and bored. What Jodi may have lacked in looks comparable to the rest of the Proud Crowd—she was a little thick around the waist, and her nose was oddly turned up—she made up for in bitchiness. Dev said she was overcompensating for her insecurities, but whatever the motivations for her mean streak were didn't matter—I feared I was in for a heavy dose.

"Katie," Jodi whispered, as she slid up next to Gretchen, "listen, I don't want to sound rude, but the party is PC-only now, so maybe your mom can pick you up. I saw her earlier in the PT Cruiser, right?"

I felt the heat rise in my cheeks. PC was an acronym for

Proud Crowd. My mouth opened, but nothing came out. Besides, what could I have said? It was a one-punch knockout for Jodi. Her victim: me.

Gretchen let out a little laugh and then turned on her four-inch heels and headed back to the house. As soon as she crossed inside, she looked back my way and mouthed, "Bye."

I gritted my teeth and gave her my best fake smile.

Jodi closed the door behind her, leaving me standing alone in the dark. From within the house I heard Gretchen say it again . . . *seventy-one* . . . and then everyone laughed.

It was going to be a long walk home.

CHAPTER

2

UNLIKE GRETCHEN'S veritable castle, Chez Winthrop was a bungalow-style, two-story house in West Millbank. You could drive by the aging, yellow clapboard siding and wraparound porch without giving it a second look—but hey, it was home. Pretty much the cliché of the absent-minded college professor (he taught Literary Theory at NYU), Dad wasn't one for home improvements; but a few years back, Mom had convinced him to renovate the first floor. While the upstairs is still a bit of a rabbit warren of bedrooms and closets, the redesigned downstairs has an open layout—the humongo kitchen flowing into the requisite family room with oversized sofas, all of which lead to the porch via newly installed French doors. It's a great place to hang out when you have friends over—but if you're looking for privacy, you're out of luck.

By 9:30 a.m., I was sitting downstairs at the breakfast table and desperate for the Sunday morning cup of coffee my mom usually brewed for me. Unfortunately I was still empty-handed because my mother was on the phone and preoccupied with the star of her life, my sister, Melissa. A model of impossibly perky, preppie perfection, back in her day at Millbank High, Mel had been the junior-class president (opted out of the running her senior year), dated the captain of the soccer team (please, no comments), and now, just like Mom had, was running for president of her sorority (sororities—gag!) at Wake Forest. So when my sister calls, whether it's 9:00 a.m. on a Sunday or 3:00 a.m. on a Tuesday, the world stops. I could be on the side of the highway with a flat tire in a blizzard at midnight, but if my sister's number came up on the caller ID, my parents would drop me like yesterday's news.

"Wow, honey, he sounds great," Mom said into the phone as she glanced over at me. "And he's going to Harvard Business School next year?"

I got up to make my own coffee, but she waved at me to sit down. I rolled my eyes in annoyance.

"No sugar, right?" she mouthed as she nodded her head, listening to my sister blather on.

"One big one, please," I said, louder than necessary.

She sighed and placed my coffee in front of me. While she walked around the kitchen, checking for dust (she was a little OCD about cleaning) and yacking with my sister, I cradled the warm mug and stared at the wall, feeling lousy about myself. Lying wide awake in my bed, I'd spent the better part of the wee hours of the morning replaying my conversation with Will in my head—*why had I acted like such a retard?!*—and trying to make sense of what Gretchen said—*what the hell did "seventy-one" mean anyway?* And then there was the big question: If Gretchen hadn't invited me to the party, who had?

"So how was the party last night?" my mom asked. Lost in my own thoughts, I hadn't noticed that she'd hung up the phone.

"Fine," I said, now putting my nose in the Sunday Style section of the *New York Times.*

"Did you and Gretchen talk?"

Now, your average mom would've asked if I'd met any boys, how I'd gotten home, if anyone was drinking, etc., but it had been clear from the moment I mentioned the invitation to Gretchen's party that my mom had her own interests at heart. She was hoping for a bridge to Gretchen's mom, Abby Tanner—the one feat of social maneuvering that even Mel the Magnificent hadn't managed to accomplish. Abby Tanner is *the* Abby Tanner, the jewelry designer, whose earrings were most recently seen on Alicia Keys at the

Grammy Awards. Mr. Tanner's no slouch, either; he was a big Wall Street money guy and was the one who'd financed the start-up of Abby's company. Yeah, the Tanners, like their daughter, are what you'd call "big" in town. Long story short, for Mom, this party represented our family's first invitation to be included in the exclusive circle of Tanner friends.

"So did you talk to her?" she repeated.

She was trying to sound casual, like she didn't really care, but needless to say, I knew better. I decided to spare her my not-actually-invited-to-the-party humiliation. Trust me, it would've been worse for her than me.

"Not really," I said. "It was kind of loud."

She gave me a hard little look, as if to say, "Spill the beans."

"She said 'Hi' and 'Bye,'" I snipped. "We're not suddenly BFF if that's what you're hoping."

"What's BFF?"

Oh, c'mon.

"Never mind."

"Did you at least make an effort to talk to her?" she pressed. "You know we have our interview for the club coming up, and her parents—"

The Millbank Country Club. *Well, of course.* That's all my mother had been able to talk about for the last year, and despite the fact that Dad and I thought it was all really stupid, she had applied for membership. There were a million hoops you had to jump through—references, nominations, and some big-deal interview—but, like some desperate freshman boy, my mother was falling all over herself to get in. Gretchen's dad was on the board and Abby Tanner ran the selection committee, so you get the picture.

"—her parents would be really helpful for making things go smoothly."

"Mom, please leave me out of it."

"We're applying as a family. Our meeting with the club manager is in two weeks."

God, the woman is relentless.

I rolled my eyes, got up, and crossed to the island, where I grabbed half a bagel from the basket. Out of the corner of my eye, I could feel my mother watching me, holding her breath, so I took a glob of cheese and put it directly into my mouth. I could sense her blood pressure ticking up a few points, but this morning she deserved it.

Not that she ever would've admitted it, but I knew my mom wanted me to be more like Mel. I'm sure she stayed up late at night wondering how her daughters could've been so different. I mean, I wasn't a complete zero, but I didn't go out of my way to climb the social ladder at Millbank, either.

"Are you going shopping with the girls today?" Mom asked, changing the subject, probably in a desperate attempt to lessen my calorie intake.

"Maybe."

"You're just full of information, Katie."

The sarcasm noted, it was my turn to give her a hard little look. I made mine extra hard because she was being extra obnoxious.

"You don't want to buy anything you're not going to fit in," she noted.

Did I mention she was passive-aggressive also?

"If it doesn't fit, I'll throw on some of those shoulder pads you wore in the eighties—they made you look thin, right?"

It bugged her when I trashed the eighties, but let's be honest, there has never been a decade more ripe for trashing than the decade that brought us A Flock of Seagulls and *Porky's*.

"I just always hoped you'd get to go to the Black & White—like Melissa," she said, getting up and pouring the last of her coffee into the sink. She just had to bring up the Black & White thing, didn't she? The Black & White, for those of you from outside the greater Millbank area, was this huge yearly gala, but more on this later.

"Can we just drop it, please?!"

My mother pursed her lips and brought her hand to her forehead. She said nothing for a moment. "You know I'm only concerned because I love you, honey, right?"

"Totally understand, Mom," I answered, suddenly feeling guilty that I'd yelled at her. I knew deep down that she probably meant well. "But you know there are worse things in the world than my not going to the B & W."

Not that I foresaw that happening . . . even if there were no prospects yet.

"I know, sweetie. And if I can help in any way—"

"Mom!" I walked behind her and squeezed her shoulder. "Everything's going to be okay."

At least that's what I was hoping.

CHAPTER

3

EVERY SUNDAY, Dev, Callie, and I had brunch at Cozy Corner in what passed for downtown in East Millbank. Our brunch had become a ritual ever since Callie passed her driver's test two years before. She was actually a year older than me and Dev, because her parents had taken her to India for a year when they did Doctors Without Borders. Her mom was a big deal in the medical world—she was one of the first African American women to perform open-heart surgery—and she was always traveling to developing countries to train local doctors in the latest methods and treatments. Our brunch was really just an excuse to pore over everything that had gone down during the week: whether it was school gossip, parental drama, or anything boy-related. Although the geriatric crowd was often bumbling around, slurping prune juice, and waddling to the restrooms, we mostly had the place to ourselves, so we felt comfortable unpacking what needed to be unpacked.

When I walked in, Callie and Dev were already there, chatting away.

"Kate, sit down here," Callie said, patting the seat next to her. "So what happened last night?"

"Spill it." Dev grinned.

Callie, Dev, and I were different in our own ways, but we were close as close could be. If I had to choose two people in the world to count on—for like the rest of my life—I'd pick Dev and Cal. We'd been through it all together: first kisses, the SAT, college applications, even Dev's parents' divorce. Nothing meant more to me than our friendship. My invitation to Gretchen's party had mystified the three of us, and while it was clear Dev was a little jealous, they'd both pushed me to go.

"So what happened?" Dev pressed again.

"Nada."

"It's never nada with you," Callie said.

I winced and looked out the window. "Can't we talk about something else first?"

The girls glanced at each other, and a moment later, Callie reached out and grabbed my hand, clutching it between her palms. Of the three of us, Callie was the natural mother. At nearly six feet tall with an Afro that made her appear six-three, Callie was bigger than life. Beautiful, ethereal, and blessed with a natural instinct for fashion, she had earned her nickname "Miss Fabulous" ten times over. Let me put it this way: Callie probably could've been part of Gretchen's clique, but her moral compass was too strong to be involved in the evil one's silly games.

"C'mon. It couldn't have been that bad," she whispered, like I was her little baby. "But tell me everything, otherwise I'm heading home, because I didn't get up before noon on a Sunday just to listen to you say 'nada.'"

"Okay," I relented. "Turns out I wasn't really invited."

"WHAT?" Dev shrieked.

I leaned on the wood veneer table and proceeded to give them the blow-by-blow on what initially had happened (or for that matter, did not happen) at the party: wandering the house, studying the books, and desperately trying to blend in. Then I told them about my convo with Gretchen on the front lawn. Their eyes went wide.

"Omigod, that's harsh. Do you think she was lying?" Callie asked.

"Why would she lie?"

They both were silent for a beat.

"Either way," Dev observed, "the girl's a grade-A bitch. She didn't have to rub your face in it."

Dev and I had been friends since the seventh grade, but if you saw us side by side you never would have pegged us as such. For starters, we looked nothing alike. She was short, had dirty-blond hair, and was kind of *academic* looking (in middle school, she'd been voted most likely to be a bookworm by a bunch of mean boys, and I don't think she'd ever recovered socially or psychologically). I was a tall brunette, without any obviously definable drawbacks or advantages, if you catch my drift. But it was our personalities where we really diverged. I was somewhat quiet and prone to thinking too long before I spoke, whereas she was a neurotic attack dog high on NoDoz. Despite it all, we had an unbreakable bond, and Callie, always the one to dabble in Eastern philosophy, said Dev was the yin to my yang.

"And then, what was even more bizarre," I continued, forging on to the bitter end, "is that Gretchen called me 'Seventy-one.'"

"What's that?" Callie frowned.

"Gretchen said, 'Will likes to slum, Seventy-one.'"

Dev sat straight up. "Hold on a second. Did you talk to Will B.?!"

A smile crept across my face.

"Will B.!" Dev yelled.

"Now, that's why I got up this morning!" Callie chimed in.

"What did he say?"

I grinned and leaned back into my seat. It wasn't every day that you get to say that you were hanging out with Will

B. "Okay, so I was getting beer from the keg, and he sort of rolled up."

"At the keg." Callie smiled. "A classic guy move."

But Dev didn't flinch. Where Dev and I *were* similar was in our lack of success with boys. I think our combined record was four for thirty-one, and that—though I'm loath to admit this—included the occasional date with an underclassman. Totally on the down low, I don't think she'd ever even kissed a boy. Virgin lips were rare these days, but Dev had them. Some day when she met a boy as smart as she was, I knew the rockets would go off, but until then she had me and Callie.

"So he had this wild look in his eyes, like maybe he was on something. It was so sexy. He took my cup and started pumping the keg up, and then he sort of mumbled something extraordinary."

"What?!!" they shouted in unison.

I cracked up. I'd never seen the two them so worked up over a little boy story. Tears started to roll down my cheeks and my stomach was cramping from laughing so hard. Callie and Dev started laughing too, and eventually the waitress had to come over and offer us water.

"Okay, okay," I finished. "He said: 'You were always the one I couldn't see.'"

"Wow," Callie breathed.

Dev's eyes lit up.

"What?" I said, turning to Dev.

"Nothing," she said. "But it was only a matter of time."

Callie seemed to catch her vibe, because suddenly she nodded, too. "That's right."

"What's right?" I asked. I had no idea what Dev was talking about, but it was weirding me out.

"Anyway, he took off and then, like, the party emptied out in two seconds. Will practically evaporated before my eyes. That's when the whole Gretchen thing went down."

"Well, no wonder she was bitchy to you," Dev concluded. "She was pissed that you were talking to Will. You know she's always had a thing for him. "

"They dated," Callie said. "For like a millisecond—I heard he dumped her after they did the deed."

"Couldn't have happened to a more evil creature," Dev said.

The thought of Will B. getting down with Gretchen silenced everyone, and then our food came, and the subject drifted to Mexico and our senior summer trip. As the three of us started talking about where we were going to stay, the flight down, and whether there'd be time to visit the Mayan ruins, I felt a wave of nostalgia wash over me. How many more brunches were the three of us going to have together? How many more late-night hangouts before I was in Rhode Island (early admission to Brown, thank you very much),

Dev was in New York, and Callie was all the way out at Berkeley? The more I thought about the future, the more I thought about the past. Things I might have done differently. How high school was, once and for all, truly coming to an end.

Before I knew it, an hour had passed and Callie had to take off for her yoga class. While we waited for change from the waitress, Dev got up and went to the powder room.

Deep down, I knew I should just let it go, but something wouldn't let me.

"Cal," I said, "what did Dev mean before when she said it was only a matter of time?"

Callie stared at me for a few seconds. "You don't know, do you? If I hadn't known you this long, I wouldn't believe it."

"What?" I said, starting to feel self-conscious, like there was something wrong with me.

Callie got up from the booth and flung her yoga mat over her back. She kissed me on the cheek and let her beautiful, long, elegant fingers rest against my cheek.

"You're beautiful, inside and out," she said.

"Thanks." I blushed, not knowing what else to do.

"I mean it, K," she said. "The only difference between you and Gretchen is that she believes she is."

"Right."

"I'm serious." And then she pinched my cheek, like a

grandmother would. She walked away with a smile so big that it held all that was right in the world.

I wanted to *believe* what she just told me—that soon my Friday nights wouldn't only be spent with my girlfriends or alone with my dog—but I couldn't. In the mirror across the room I was still that little girl who always thought of herself as too boring, too brainy, and too wrong for any boy to like, never mind love.

CHAPTER

4

AFTER SCHOOL on Mondays and Wednesdays, and every other Sunday, I worked at The Millbank BookStop. When you walk through the door of the BookStop, the store's owner, Mrs. Sawyer, is always waiting to greet you so she can place the book she knows you'd want to read right in your hands. Sure, the place was a little unique—what with its oddball customers, dusty shelves, and quirky manager, Howie (Mrs. Sawyer's freaky-but-cool, forty-four-year-old son), who always sat perched on his stool by the door reading a dog-eared copy of Marx's *Communist Manifesto*—but despite it all, the four-foot-eleven turbocharged granny, who was born during the Depression, had a thriving business because the people of Millbank consider her and her little store a town treasure.

When I woke up that morning, I imagined finishing brunch and coming to the BookStop and working on the graduation window. Unlike stores that just put the stacks of bestsellers in the window, the BookStop windows are thematic. You might see one filled with a beach towel, a sand pail, and a bunch of books about boats, cruises, summertime, and a pile of thrillers, mysteries, and romantic "beach reads." Or a battered stockpot might be surrounded by wooden spoons and two hundred cookbooks. The themes are sometimes seasonal, but not always, and Mrs. Sawyer prefers not to repeat.

I hadn't always been such a fan of Mrs. Sawyer—she could be a bit of a tough cookie—but back in February of my junior year, after I'd spent nine months shelving books, Mrs. Sawyer asked me if I'd design a window for Valentine's Day. As much of an honor as it was to be asked to design a window, I wasn't dating anybody at the time—how shocking!—and to be honest, I was feeling like a little, bitter Miss Lonelyhearts.

"I don't think I'd make a very nice window, Mrs. Sawyer," I said. "I hate Valentine's Day."

"Here's an idea," she growled. "Make it for all the broken hearts in Millbank." She paused for a few moments, then said, "Use black hearts and make sure *Anna Karenina* is front and center."

And just like that, she disappeared into the back office,

leaving me with a window to design. I'd tried to sulk my way out of doing it, but she'd turned the tables on me. I ended up putting together an outrageous display with hanging black hearts surrounded by books about the worst breakups in the history of literature. *Madame Bovary. The Great Gatsby. Romeo and Juliet.*

From that day on, I knew Mrs. Sawyer was a go-to gal. We all have them—our "work mom" or "school mom"—the older woman who has some wisdom about the world, kind of like your own mom but minus all the baggage.

That afternoon, as I sat there trying to create a graduation window, I didn't need a listener. What I wanted was some peace and quiet, some time to think. In six short weeks, I'd be gliding by Mom and Dad in cap and gown as Mr. Johnson read the lyrics to "Turn the Page" by Bob Seger (it was an insane Millbank tradition started in the seventies and kept up for some inexplicable reason), and then none of this would matter. Not Gretchen, not my mother's harping, not my pathetic life.

I glanced out the window and watched a Hummer pull to a stop on the other side of the street. All four doors popped open, and a gaggle of Proud Crowd members— Elisa, Jodi, Carrie, and others—gaily poured out, heads bobbing, eyes sparkling. I watched them for a few moments and tried to imagine what their lives were like. I couldn't imagine that the smell of old books permeated their clothes or that they ever spent a Saturday night alone.

"Where are you today, Miss Kate?" Mrs. Sawyer suddenly said, standing behind me.

I turned around to see her staring at me over her glasses.

"Sorry, Mrs. Sawyer," I said. "I'm a little out of it today. I've got a lot going on."

"Something you want to talk about?" she asked. Her voice was like gravel from sixty years of smoking.

"No, just tired from studying late."

"On Saturday night, in April?" she questioned. "The rest of your friends stopped studying a couple of months ago."

I looked at her and wondered how she kept so sharp. Clearly her bullshit radar was finely tuned to my bull.

"Can I change the window on Wednesday? I just don't feel inspired today. The idea of graduating, leaving my friends, has me down," I sort of lied.

"All right. You do what you have to do. Wednesday is fine with me." She looked at her watch. "Howie hired somebody new. You can show him the ropes—Howie's no good at that."

I was more than happy to take her up on the offer, because I actually liked training new people. Besides, maybe walking someone through the store would get my mind off my problems.

"So who's the new victim?" I asked.

Howie was sitting on his bar stool, his nose practically

touching the book he was reading. When standing, which wasn't often when on the job, he was about six feet three, weighed no less than three hundred pounds, and had a bright red Afro. Mrs. Sawyer was African American and her late husband was Jewish, so I guess that's just how the genes blended. He looked up and pointed behind me.

I turned around to see who he was pointing at, and my eyes narrowed ever so slightly in surprise. It was Jack Clayton. Out of instinct, my eyes darted about looking for Will B., but the Boy Wonder was without Batman. I'd never really taken Jack Clayton in before. He had dirty-blond hair, a strong chin, and dark chocolate eyes flecked with green. He stood about six feet tall with a gentle slouch that bordered on awkward. From what I'd heard, he wasn't much of a talker.

"Jack."

"Hey," he said. "Good throwdown last night."

I nodded.

"You work here, huh," he mumbled. "Is it cool?"

I looked over at Howie and smiled. "Yeah, it is."

"All right, then."

We stood there for a few moments not saying anything. I mean, what was I supposed to do—boss Jack Clayton around?

"Anyway, I'm going to train you," I blurted out.

"Train me," he said. "Like Shamu."

"No, not like Shamu," I said, flustered. "They train Shamu with fish—I'm going to train you with free books."

"Free books," he said. "Right—I could get used to that."

"All employees get one free book a month and fifty percent discount on all others."

"Nice," he said. So Jack Clayton was a reader—a nice little surprise.

"Best part of the job," I continued. "So why are you taking a job with a month of school left?"

"To be close to you," he said, and his face was stone serious. My heart stopped beating for all of a second, and then a smile crossed his face. "Just kidding. Dad said I needed to kick in some money for college—you know, I'm learning the value of a dollar and all that."

"I see," I said. *Get out the violins—another rich kid sent to the salt mines.*

I spent the next hour giving Jack a tour of the BookStop and showing him "the ropes." The store was long and had three floors. On the first floor we kept all the new releases along with mysteries, thrillers, graphic novels, and comic books. On the top floor we kept our academic sections, stuff like philosophy, lit crit, and history. In the basement we had our more risqué section for women—romance and erotica. I was kind of skeezed out by it all, but it sure did sell. As I walked Jack around, he nodded mostly and occasionally asked a question, so it was a little hard to tell if he was picking everything up or if he was just planning on quitting the moment his first shift ended.

By the end of my shift I was so bushed from talking that I grabbed the largest cart of unstacked books I could find and started to show him how to shelve them by subject and author.

"How's the band?" I said, offhand. I was fishing for Will scoop, but I tried to make the question seem casual.

"Good. We're playing the Electric next Saturday—you should come."

"Uh—sure."

Just the thought of Will B. all sweaty and on stage made my heart swoon.

"Cool," he said. Jack picked up a copy of some poems by Allen Ginsberg and showed it to me. "Have you read the Beats?"

"No. Are they good?"

"*Were* good, but I mean out-of-their-friggin'-minds good," he said. "Don't tell me you haven't read 'Howl'?"

I shook my head and bit down on my lower lip. I took pride in having read books nobody else had, and now here was this boy making me feel like a reading lightweight. "No, I haven't."

Jack smiled and looked down at the book in his hand. "Here, take this—I'm giving you my first free book of the month."

"Thanks," I said, trying to sound normal. *Is Jack Clayton flirting with me?*

Just then Howie called my name over the PA system. I told Jack to finish stacking, and I tucked the book under my arm and walked to the front of the store.

"What do you think of the poem 'Howl'?" I asked Howie as I waited for him to give me another cart of books to stack.

"Brilliant poem," he replied, "but Ginsberg played the same note for too long."

"Fidel," I began—Howie and I liked to joke that I was Che Guevara and he was Fidel Castro at the beginning of the revolution—"our new comrade . . . he's a big fan of the Beats and he's donating his first free book to me." I held it up.

Howie scratched his goatee. It was a mixture of white, gray, and red, and it made him look like an old-time sixties radical.

"Is this comrade going to stack books or give them away?" he asked. "Because the revolution doesn't need a hero—it needs a good book stacker."

I looked back and Jack was reading—I guessed his head and mind were in another universe, and for a moment I envied him. There was nothing I would've liked more than to drop away into another world right then.

"I think he'll be a good, slow stacker, Fidel."

"Revolutions," Howie mused, "don't happen overnight. We'll give him a chance."

CHAPTER

5

BY TEN O'CLOCK, the Sunday-night blues set in. The bleak wasteland of an entire week of stupefyingly boring school stretched ahead of me like an endless desert highway.

In the hopes of staving off a trip to the freezer for a bowl of Chunky Monkey ice cream (this monk needed no more chunk!), I changed into my comfy sweats, donned the cheesy pink cowboy hat I'd won at Six Flags a few years back, and hopped online to check the status of a bunch of things I was auctioning.

I'd built a little business selling things out of my parents' attic. My mom was a pack rat, and Dad had been after her to get rid of some stuff forever, so when I suggested the idea, he was more than happy for me to turn her old Thighmaster, their ABBA records (who even owns a record player anymore?), and even his red lava lamp (this I actually kept for myself) into some cold, hard cash. Don't get me wrong, I wasn't making big bucks or anything . . . twenty bucks here, fifty bucks there . . . but it was enough to pay my monthly iTunes bill and, in a good month, fund a few trips to the mall.

I was just about to call Dev for a chat when my IM window popped up. I clicked over to it.

MikeMilken: Do you want to know?

Okay . . . that's creepy.

Who was Mike Milken? I searched my mind, trying to place the name, but I was drawing a total blank. School? The BookStop? Somebody I'd met online? Mystified, I grabbed the Millbank school directory, but there were no Milkens in it.

I sat back down. Two could play at that game.

KK: Know what?

MikeMilken: What the Market is? You're number seventy-one.

I literally froze at my computer, just staring at the words.

Seventy-one. Yes, I desperately wanted to know, but I also wasn't so sure I wanted anything to do with this freak who was IMing me so late at night.

Just as I was about to respond, there was a knock at my door, and I hid the IM window on my desktop. My dad poked his head in.

"Ice cream?" he said.

Try as I might, the world was conspiring against me.

"Sure."

He came in and put the bowl on my dresser. "What're you doing?"

Ever since my dad read an article about online predators, he liked to periodically drop in during the "dangerous times," e.g., IMing after ten p.m. Generally speaking, I appreciated the gesture, but tonight I was actually about to communicate with one of those weirdos and I wanted to be left alone.

"Busy talking to Dev."

"Oh, what's she up to?"

I turned around from my desk and gave him the I-love-you-but-please-leave-me-alone face. He was pretty sensitive to that expression and shuffled out with a little wave. I grabbed the ice cream and returned to my computer.

The IM signal dinged again:

MikeMilken: theMillbankmarket.com/
password: hedgefund

In a flash, I scribbled the address and password down on a Post-it, and a moment later, Mike Milken (whoever he was) logged off. By now, my hands were trembling a little, and I struggled to type the new address into Explorer. Once I did, I hit return, and sure enough the password screen came up.

What the hell was this?

I typed in "hedgefund" and pushed ENTER. The screen went blank for a few moments, and a fear that I'd just downloaded the worst virus of all time swept over me; but a few seconds later, a new window opened.

THE MILLBANK SOCIAL STOCK MARKET

My eyes went wide and I took a big scoop of ice cream.

It certainly wasn't the most elaborate Web site I'd ever been on—it was pretty basic, actually. Blue background, white writing . . . that was it. The person who built the site was obviously no computer genius, and I mentally crossed off the mathletes as possible suspects.

I scrolled down from the top of the page, and there was a message.

WELCOME TO THE MARKET
Below are the valuations as of 4/19

I didn't get it.

I scrolled down some more, still trying to figure out what it was exactly. It looked like a page from the Stock Index of the *Wall Street Journal*. There was a long ranking of what I assumed to be stock symbols and their end-of-day trading value. Next to each symbol was a one-line analysis. The first twenty stocks were in a bracket that said BLUE CHIPS.

Why would someone be giving me stock advice? I mean, what was wrong with the world that people in high school were suddenly trading stock tips?

But the more I studied it, the more the oddities started to jump out at me. First of all, there weren't any companies I recognized. To be sure, I'm no money guru, and I've never really studied the stock market, but I certainly know what a blue-chip stock is—it's a stock everyone wants to own. GE, Microsoft, and Google, these were classic Blue Chippers, but none of them were anywhere to be found. As I began looking at the sheet more closely, I noticed some of the lingo seemed very unprofessional and young. Things like, "This stock's brain-to-body ratio is way off," or "Investment high, her return is low." Since when are companies referred to as *her*? Isn't that only for boats?

Gradually I focused on the number-one-ranked stock. It was called GRT Inc. and next to it was written: "Deep pockets needed, but the package is everything you dreamed of." That's when it dawned on me. G-R-T. This wasn't an acronym for a publicly traded company, they were initials. GRT stood for Gretchen Rachel Tanner.

What I was looking at was a ranking.

The ranking of every girl in the senior class!

Holy sh—!

Quickly I scanned the rest of the list. Number two: ETE.

Elisa Estrada, of course.

Not much of a surprise there, either.

Three through six were pretty much what I would've expected—more members of the Proud Crowd—and I began scrolling down through the names, looking for mine. Different sets of numbers had different subheadings: 20–40: Preferred Stock, 41–60: Penny Stock, 61–140: Junk Bonds.

I scrolled down.

And down.

And down. I suddenly wondered if I was even listed.

Until I finally saw my initials. I was right above Hester Schultz.

71. KCW—currently valued at $1.75 a share.
Change since last week: -3

Oh. My. God.

I didn't exactly know what the change part was, but I definitely knew what it meant to be ranked seventy-first out of the 140 girls in my class. I was just on the wrong side of the great divide. Was I that much of a loser?! Tears formed in the corners of my eyes, and I took another big bite of ice cream; and just when I thought it couldn't get any worse, I noticed that there was an icon of a bear flashing next to my name. Moving the cursor over, I clicked on it. A new window opened. And if the list part was horrifying, this new page was truly mortifying.

It was a whole dossier.

About me.

My photograph from last year's yearbook was posted in the top right corner—did I really look that bad?—and listed next to it were all my activities: my job at the BookStop, what courses I was taking, where I was going to college, how I got to school in the morning. It was crazy! To the left of my picture, there was a chart that tracked my ranking week by week (it was pretty much flat). Underneath my photo, there was a box titled INSIDER INFORMATION. It looked like a blog for market players where they could randomly contribute commentary on what individual girls were doing.

4/18 Seen at GT's shindig—who invited her?!
4/15 Stuffing
4/15 Is her chest getting bigger or is she stuffing?
4/11 Wiped out in the cafeteria—lol!

This was bad. Really bad. Had I wiped out in the cafeteria? Yes. Was I stuffing my bra? NO! I took my last spoonful of ice cream, and then, as I was thinking there couldn't be anything worse, I scrolled down to a box at the very bottom of the screen where there was a flashing star.

KCW LLC.

MARKET RANKING: 71
TODAY'S CHANGE: ↓3

SHARE PRICE: $1.75
   CHANGE: ↓0.06 (-0.09%)
L/B RATIO: 2.3
3-MONTH RANGE: $1.23 – $1.81
STATUS: JUNK BOND

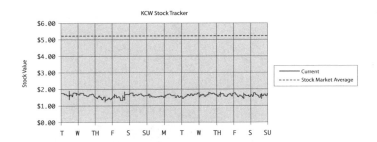

KCW Stock Tracker

ANALYST RECOMMENDATION: has promise, but continues to show no interest in improving her l/b (looks-to-brains) ratio. A date night would probably yield a low R.O.I. (Return on Investment). The smart investor stays away.

DEFINITE SELL

CHAPTER

6

IT WAS A dark night.

I spent hours poking around the Market, checking out other girls' dossiers, poring over the rankings, and looking at my page over and over. Eventually I found Dev (she was worse off than me, No. 121) and Callie (she probably couldn't care less, but was No. 11), and much as I tried to brush the whole thing off and chock it up to a bad joke, I couldn't let it go. I mean, there it was—in black and white. It was undeniable. If what the Market said was true, I was what somebody with tact might call "below average." Don't get me wrong, I'd never had any illusions of being the It Girl, but to have it laid out for you before your very eyes is a whole other matter.

So what did I do when I discovered I was two notches

above chopped liver? Hide in my closet and skip the last six weeks of school?

No.

Hell, no.

I was a Winthrop, and my dad always told me that a Winthrop takes life head on.

For the first time in about two years, I woke up before my alarm went off. As I pushed myself out of bed at 5:30 a.m., Remington (my cocker spaniel) looked up at me from the corner like I was crazy, but I was feeling uncommonly energized. There were so many things to do and so little time to do them. Reaching deep into my closet, I pulled out a cute J. Crew dress that I'd accidentally put in the dryer a few years back and had shrunk. It was now a little too short and a little too tight, but tight in the right places, I hoped. After a quick trip to the laundry room to iron out a wrinkle, I hit the shower, dried my hair, and dug out the curling iron from underneath my bathroom sink. By eight o'clock my hair was looking as good as it ever had, and I'd managed to hide the big circles under my eyes from two sleepless nights with some heavy-duty concealer I'd snagged from my mom's vanity. After a few final touches—some Mac lip gloss and my jean jacket—I checked everything in the mirror one last time, and—if I may say so myself—I was looking pretty damn good.

It was going to be a good day. I just knew it.

* * *

But as soon as I set foot in school, my newfound grit disappeared. I'm not sure what triggered it, but by the end of first period I started feeling like my old self. The self that was seventy-first on the Market. Whether it was nearly breaking an ankle in my three-inch heels on my way to homeroom; or that the dress I was wearing *was* in fact way too small and I was pretty sure I looked fat; or simply a Pavlovian response to being back in the building where I had drowned in anonymity for four years, I don't know for sure, but my quick fix to popularity was turning into a quick trip to Depressionville. I felt more like a seventy-one than ever before.

How could I have thought that two hours of primping was going to change anything? I mean, who was I kidding? I was Kate Winthrop—smart girl, a little geeky, with a good heart. That's all I'd ever be, at least while I was still at Millbank. Who's to say how many people logged on to the Market every day? How many people were judging me on a daily basis—breaking down what I was wearing, who I was talking to, how I was behaving? It didn't matter really. There was no escaping it. Maybe once I got to Brown I could change into someone different, someone cool, someone sought after, someone different. Perhaps once I got to a place where my history as a social nonentity wasn't so well documented, I could shed my old skin, but until then, it was simply better to lay low. Blend in. Stay with the pack. What's that old saying? It's the tall blade of grass that gets cut? Well I didn't need—or want—any more wounds.

By the middle of seventh period, I was thinking about one thing: get through Econ Class, go home, and disappear into the old Katie Winthrop. While Dev stood in the front of the room giving her final presentation—something to do with the big bang theory of branding—I found myself gazing across the room at Gretchen and her coterie of It Friends, silently wondering to myself what made them cool, and me not. Elisa Estrada was Number Two on the Market. She was blessed with wavy brown hair, beautiful blue eyes, and a genuine warmth that won everyone over, including the ice princess Gretchen. Jodi Letz—Number Six—hardly a natural beauty, and known in parts of the county as Jodi "Lets-me," was ranked high purely by her association with the Proud Crowd. And then there was Gretchen. Sure, there were the obvious things that marked her for Number One: she was beautiful, her dad was a big wheel and all that, and rumor had it she wasn't too shy when it came to a late-night tango with the boys . . . but there had to be something else.

While my analytical mind (2180 on my SAT) worked overtime on the alchemy of popularity, I still couldn't make the math add up. There must have been some variable, some innate quality she possessed that lesser lights of the social universe like me did not. Was it something she learned from her mom—if so, why hadn't *my* mom taught me the secret handshake—or was it simply something that she'd been blessed with by the genetic lottery? Was there some regimen that I could undergo to transform me from a toadette into a princess?

Get it together, Kate!!

I took a deep breath and tried to clear my mind. This isn't who you are, I told myself. You don't care about empty things like popularity. You're above it all. You are your own person.

Right?

But no matter what I said to myself, no matter how many of those corny platitudes I managed to summon to my mind, the Market was still there. I couldn't get it out of my head. Seemingly overnight, I'd been transformed from a girl who felt like she knew her place in the world to a shivering bag of nerves.

"Kate? Are you with us?"

Blood rushed to my cheeks. Mr. Walsh was standing over my desk, and the whole class was staring at me.

"Sorry?" I whispered. Behind me, some guy chortled.

"Please pay attention, Kate," Mr. Walsh said, shaking his head.

Mr. Walsh was a Millbank alum who had come back to teach after making a lot of dough on Wall Street. Why he left Wall Street was beyond me, but he said he wanted to give something back to the community. My mom said he was noble, but Dad said he was perhaps a little foolish, too. We all considered ourselves pretty lucky to have him, because he was probably the best teacher in the school. He was tough and demanding, and though we complained, we knew he was pushing us to be as good as we could be. And that's priceless in my book.

"I was asking you what you thought of Dev's conclusion that the marketing of a product is more important than the quality of the product itself," he said. "Care to comment?"

"I think she's right," I mumbled. Mr. Walsh stared at me, and I searched my mind for something more appropriate to say, but he quickly turned to Gretchen.

"A dud's a dud," she tossed out. "Like when Coke tried to launch New Coke. You can't fake quality. It's like being beautiful—I mean, you either are or you aren't, right? You can't convince people that something is true just by telling them it is."

She looked really impressed with herself after she finished what I suspected was the first real thought she'd ever had. I glanced up at Dev, who was now beaming at me to counter.

"What about President Bush?" I said.

"What about him?" Mr. Walsh inquired.

"Didn't he have us all believing that they had WMDs

in Iraq?" I said, and then looked directly at Gretchen. "And his brain, didn't we believe he had one?"

The class erupted into laughter.

Mr. Walsh motioned for the class to settle down, and he walked back toward Dev, who looked very pleased by my challenge to Gretchen's argument.

"I think Miss Tanner and Miss Winthrop, in their own unique ways, are both correct. If you examine . . ."

But as Mr. Walsh waxed on about focus groups, case studies, and polling, I found the Market intruding on my mind once more, and one question kept popping up:

Who was behind it?

The person orchestrating the Market could be *anyone*. It could be a student or a teacher, or it could be a hundred students working together. He, she, them—whoever it was could be sitting in this very room. Suddenly the room was filled with perps, so I started eliminating suspects one by one. Jason Sanders was too lazy, Jeff Briggs was too stupid, the posse of skateboard dudes didn't give a crap. But I had a few clues, too: whoever kept the dossier was probably at Gretchen's party and possibly a member of this class, because we all filtered in from sixth period lunch (the scene of my aforementioned wipeout). Given that Gretchen had been the one to mention it all in the first place, I made a mental note: when class ended, I would watch her and her minions. If they were behind the Market—or at least the people contributing to my dossier—I was sure they'd be keeping close tabs on me.

When the bell rang, I lingered in my chair fiddling with my backpack zipper. It wasn't broken, but I needed camouflage while I observed others.

"Need some help?" said a now familiar voice. I looked up into the dreamy blue eyes of Will B., and next to him my new work buddy, Jack Clayton.

"Yeah, it's stuck," I lied.

Will took my bag and with a quick yank he opened it up.

"Oh, thanks," I said. "I must have been doing it wrong."

"I mastered the zipper in first grade," he said.

Great, now he's mocking me.

For the second time in my life I was talking to Will B., and for the second time in two days I was making a complete fool of myself. With Will and Jack standing side by side, you realized it was no accident that Will was the lead singer. You know how they say that movie stars have this quality where you can't help but want to look at them? Well, Will had it—and Jack didn't.

"Did you read Ginsberg?" Jack asked.

Will looked at Jack and then at me. That Jack and I had had a relationship of which he wasn't part seemed to throw Will for a loop.

"Yeah," I lied. Truth was, I'd brought the book home and intended to read some of it before I saw Jack again at work that coming Wednesday.

"Wow," said Will, as he punched Jack in the arm. "Dude, you push that wounded-poet game on every girl you meet?"

It was perhaps the single greatest exhibition of "blocking" I'd ever witnessed. "Blocking" (and that's a nice term for it) is when one boy "blocks" another from talking to a girl. There were two important facts to note in this particular case: first, a boy will only block another boy when they are both interested in a girl (me??). Second, it's often deeply painful to watch the "blocking" victim try to recover his rap after being bludgeoned the way Jack had been by Will's nifty workmanship.

Jack blushed and his mouth opened like he was about to say something, but then he looked down at his shoes.

"I'll catch you two later," Will said. "Jack—jamming at my house tonight?"

Jack chinned an "Okay."

"Bye," I said, but I wasn't even sure Will heard me.

"That wasn't true," Jack said, "what he said."

"What wasn't true?" I said, picking my bag from the desk. I was so consumed with watching Will disappear down the hall, I forgot that he had just shattered poor Jack's confidence in a single death blow.

"Never mind," Jack murmured. "I'll see you around."

I hurried down the east hall en route to my locker so I could grab my books for American Lit, but as soon as I turned the corner, I knew something was up.

A handful of guys from the soccer team were leaning against the wall snickering, and as I neared, one of the guys motioned to the others that they should take off. My pace slowed, wondering if I was missing the joke, but when I arrived at my locker, I discovered that the joke was on me.

Oh, no.

My locker number—156—had been crossed out with what looked like red lipstick. Scribbled above it, in big red letters, someone had written:

7l

Rage, horror, devastation—it all coursed through my blood. I leaped forward and started manically wiping away at the number with the arm of my jacket, trying to get it to come off. But it was useless.

It wasn't lipstick. It was permanent marker.

What had I done?! Why was I suddenly a target? Why had I been picked out to be humiliated?!

It was right then, in my most vulnerable moment—

spastically scrubbing metal, tears running down my cheeks, hair falling in my eyes—that Gretchen Tanner strolled past. She looked at me and a sly, knowing smile crept onto her face.

A hitherto unknown girl took hold of me, and I dropped my bag and stalked up to her, blocking her escape.

"Who are *you*? Who are *you*?" I stammered. "To rate people!"

"What are you talking about?" She smiled as she guided a lock of hair behind her ear.

"The numbers, the rankings. Do me a big favor and leave me out of it!" I yelled.

This time she laughed, and I think that's what pushed me over the edge. The blood drained from my face, and my fist rolled up into a ball.

"You know what?" I snapped. "I can't wait to tell everyone what you've done, because then . . . then . . . then . . . you're toast!"

Toast? Toast was my big threat? I deserved to be seventy-one if that was the best I could do.

"I'm lost here, Kate," she said.

"The Market!"

Her expression changed, slightly—softened perhaps—and she shifted her weight before adjusting her Hermès bag on her shoulder. She glanced down at her manicured nails and sighed.

"Let me give you a little piece of advice, Kate," she said.

"Don't worry about the Market, because there's nothing you can do about it."

"You can do something about it—like take me off it!"

"Me?" She squinted. "I don't have anything to do with it. I don't control it. And to be perfectly frank, I don't even know who does."

"Bull."

She shrugged her shoulders, then stared hard into my eyes. She was fierce, and I felt a chill go down my spine. "Get a clue. You think I want to be dissected on a daily basis?"

That's when I knew she wasn't lying.

I looked down at the ground, suddenly embarrassed.

"But you're Number One," I said.

She smiled condescendingly as if to communicate *Of course I am, you idiot*. Then she put her hand on my shoulder for a moment and said, "Just forget about it, Kate. It's stupid."

She paused, searching for the right words.

"You are what you are . . . and that'll never change."

CHAPTER

7

As I WALKED toward the parking lot, I felt dizzy. The hallway was spinning and suddenly every face, every set of eyes, was on me. Checking me out. Evaluating. Judging. Scoring. Every boy in the school was a potential buyer, and what I wore, what I thought, what music I listened to, mattered. I suppose every teenager felt the same anxieties at one time or another, but with the Market, my worst fears were quantified and made real and very public. I couldn't delude myself anymore by saying I was on the right side of the "pretty" fault line. No, I now knew exactly where I stood: Number Seventy-one out of 140.

In a moment of true unhappiness, I did what any red-blooded American girl in my situation would have done: I bolted. I ran straight to North Adams Street (where I parked my car for easy exiting), jumped in, and gunned it. I didn't know where I was going, but anywhere was better than MHS. Tears flowed freely, and my chest heaved with overwhelming sobs, and I felt out of control as I headed away from town.

I finally came to a stop at the Springs Reservation parking lot, overlooking all of Millbank. I'd dreamed of coming here with a boy after some mythical date, the two of us gazing at the burning lights of New York City just a few miles away. I imagined it being the most romantic night of my life, but instead I was staring at the midday smog as it slowly burned away from the hazy city skyline.

Just then my cell vibrated. Text message:

DEV: Where r u???
KATE: In hell.

Dev was the perfect person to drop some drama on. Of the two of us, I was normally even-keeled and—as I already explained—she was the neurotic psycho (her phrase, not mine), but today it was my turn to be the drama queen.

DEV: Meet me at Bucks

Starbucks was one of the few brand-name stores in the whole town of Millbank. There was a McDonald's, but it was banished to the highway and was practically inaccessible from the town itself. There was a Quiznos sub shop, a

Gap, and one or two others, but that was really it. Of the hundred or so restaurants and other merchants in town, almost all were homegrown and local. In my mind, that's what made the town great.

When I walked in, Dev had already landed us a couple of comfy chairs and two double tall skim lattes. Her laptop was open on the table, and she was reading a book, so she didn't notice me. I slowed down for a second, trying to decide what I should tell Dev. Would she understand why I was so upset? I was pretty sure she would. But then again, she was even further down the list than I was. Shouldn't I have been more concerned about her than I was about myself? Was I being a bad friend?

"Dev."

"Hey," she said, closing some book called *Freakonomics*. I looked into her eyes and immediately began to sob.

"What's wrong?" she whispered as she rubbed my back. "It's okay, Katie. Talk to me."

When I tried to speak, my throat constricted. She handed me the latte and I took a few sips, drying my eyes with the sleeve of my jean jacket.

"I'm Number Seventy-one on the Market," I said.

She got a strange look on her face. "What's the Market?"

"Somebody ranked all the girls in the senior class—it's called the Millbank Social Stock Market . . . the MSSM is what they call it."

"Yeah, so who cares?" She laughed. "It sounds goofy."

"You don't get it," I huffed. "It's online—everyone is ranked from top to bottom! It's really sophisticated."

This time Dev said nothing.

"You want to see for yourself?"

"No—it's just nonsense." She seemed annoyed, perhaps a little distracted.

"Look at it for me?"

She nodded, and I gave her the address and password. She pulled up the site in a matter of seconds, and the blue hue of the computer screen beamed off her eyes. She could read faster than anyone I knew, and scarily, she retained more, too. Her pupils ticked back and forth, like a pendulum on a clock. She seemed to be devouring the Web site. She clicked on individual girls, read the comments beneath their names, occasionally laughing or mouthing the word "Ouch," and whenever I tried to interrupt, she put her hand up and said, "Wait—one more minute."

After ten minutes, my melancholia receded, and I just became plain bored waiting for her to respond.

"So?" I said. "What do you think?"

"Honestly," she said, looking directly into my eyes. "It's totally awesome—I mean, I wish I'd thought of it."

This was so *not* the response I was expecting—or frankly wanted. Where was the outraged feminist? I wanted her to rise up like an army of Smith College undergrads ready to take back the night and tear down the chauvinist super-structure guiding these misguided pigs. I needed someone to back up my own anger, but it didn't seem to be forthcoming.

"How can you say that?"

She must have felt my disappointment, because she backtracked a little bit.

"I mean, it's total guy garbage, but you have to admit, you can't jump off once you're on. Do you know how much money we could make if we marketed this software to high schools across the nation? We'd trounce MySpace in, like, a millisecond."

Let me take a brief detour and explain Dev's response. Dev's dad is Mark Rayner, as in the founder of Dreamscape. He's worth more money than Daddy Warbucks, but don't be misled; if you met him you'd never know it. He's just one of those computer guys who made truckloads of cash, but really only ever cared about the science of it all. Ever since I've known her, Dev has been on a search for the next big thing. What drove her was hard to say, but secretly I always thought that she wanted her dad's attention, and that she thought being an entrepreneur of her own was the only way to do that. Maybe her parents' divorce had something to do with it, as well.

"Great," I said. "I can't wait to see my pathetic social status splashed all over the country."

She laughed. She actually laughed! I meant it to be funny, but not to be laughed at, if you know what I mean.

"*Your* social status!" she shouted. "What about mine? Number 121, with comments like 'I once saw her face when she actually put a book down, and it wasn't pretty.'"

Now it was my turn to laugh at something that wasn't quite as funny as she intended.

After a few minutes, we were cracking up as we pored over the commentaries on our fellow classmates. (Schadenfreude is indeed a cure for self-loathing!) Dev showed me how the stocks were traded and how values were compiled. Without boring you with too much financial mumbo jumbo, the Market was essentially an online game based around girls' popularity. Dev and I couldn't trade, see, because we weren't "traders." To be a trader, you had to have a "brokerage license," which, according to the Web site, cost five hundred dollars. Let me repeat that: just to play, you had to throw down five hundred dollars!! Once you got your license, you were given a password, a portfolio, and one-million-dollars' worth of "market money." It was a bit like Monopoly—except with stocks—and the only way a trader could increase his overall earnings was to buy stocks and hope their values rose.

"So how do you win?" I asked.

"Whoever's portfolio is worth the most come graduation takes the whole pot. With"—and she counted something on the screen—"fifty-odd portfolios, the winner stands to take away over twenty-five thousand dollars."

It was totally crazy.

"But I could win that game easily," I realized. "Why doesn't everyone just buy Gretchen's stock—her value is off the charts!"

A little smile crept across Dev's face. "It doesn't work that way. Gretchen is actually a conservative bet. Let me explain: let's say you invested all your money in Gretchen. Her stock is so high already that it's unlikely to increase in value, and frankly, it's more likely to decrease. I mean, she's gorgeous, but she's not quite Google, now is she?"

"You mean buying Gretchen is just playing it too safe?" I said.

"Right! You'll never win. The greater the risk, the greater the gain."

I was actually getting into it—I guess my econ class helped—even though I was being treated like your common pork-bellies commodity; the idea of the Market itself, I now realized, was kind of cool.

If only there were a site about the boys, I thought.

"Actually," Dev said with a smile spreading across her face, "in a perfect world, the ideal stock would be somebody just like you: pretty, totally untapped potential, and a low trading value."

"So I'm the living embodiment of the phrase, 'Buy low,

sell high.' That's great!" I said sarcastically. "I can't wait to tell Mr. Walsh."

She laughed. "Yeah, sort of, but without the high part, yet."

"Yet?"

A second, more devious, smile danced on her lips, and a dark light sparkled in her eye. "As in . . . we should play the market. We should enter."

"No way—I wouldn't bet five hundred on me."

"I would."

I cocked my head to the side and realized that Dev was already hatching a plan in her mind.

Ten minutes later, we were in Dev's attic.

Unlike her room, where her younger brother could pop in at any second—or worse, be listening in through some high-tech device (he was the true tech geek of the family)—the attic was basically impenetrable. You had to open two doors just to get to the staircase, and back in middle school, Dev had put long noisy beads midway up so it was virtually impossible to approach without us knowing. In the middle of the space there was an old-fashioned desk and a couple of antique wicker chairs. It was like going back in time, and somehow that made us feel safe.

When we first got there, Dev was like a whirling dervish. Jumping from one carton to the next, pulling out every yearbook their family had ever collected. Between her and her sister, they basically covered the last seven years at MHS, dating back to the class of 2001. I had no idea what she was looking for, but she eventually laid out all the books, opening each to a single page, dropping Post-its under the pictures of girls I only vaguely remembered.

"Beth Zupan," Dev said.

"Yeah, what about her?" I said, searching my memory banks for a little 4-1-1. "Yearbook editor when we were freshmen, right? She was a junior, I think."

"Exactly," she said. "What else do you remember about her?"

"Dark hair, green eyes, cute, but nothing to write home about. . . ."

"Right," she said. "I mean, mostly right." She turned the yearbook in my direction, and sure enough there was a picture of Beth Zupan with the Yearbook Club. I might have even used the description "dowdy."

She closed the 2003 yearbook and opened the 2004 yearbook. She turned to the back, and there was a collage of pictures titled "Spring Fling." She snapped off a Post-it and neatly placed it below the picture of a girl in a group photo with the caption, HOTTIES.

"Here," she said, sliding the book in front of me.

"What?"

"That's Beth Zupan."

I was stunned. I grabbed the old yearbook and compared the two girls. It was like an alien had inhabited the body of a yearbook editor and turned her into a Maxim swimsuit model. The conservative brown hair had been replaced by a mane of sassy blond hair, and her pasty "I stay indoors and read a lot" skin had been tanned golden. But it was more than that—she seemed to positively glow.

"This is amazing."

"That's not the half of it," Dev shouted. She grabbed the other yearbooks and showed me a series of before-and-after photos. It seemed that every year there was another girl who had come out of nowhere. Dev had even created a term for the type: the Latebloomer.

I was speechless. After an hour of looking at girls who had risen from the middle of the pack to top dog in the span of a year, Dev hit me with her theory:

"In every school, there's a girl who wallows in anonymity for three and a half years. Then, suddenly, she explodes into the consciousness of her peers," she explained. "One week she's a no one, then she goes on spring break and comes back a different girl, or suddenly one month her body changes, or the right boy notices her, and then bang, she's it and the world she'd watched from afar instantly becomes her oyster."

I said nothing for a moment. "I'm not that girl, Dev."

If I were, then anybody in school could be.

"You could be, Kate," Dev said. "And I know how to make you that girl."

"You can't tell me a tan or a haircut or a dye job is going to change my life," I snapped. "That's just make-believe."

"No, it's just good business."

"What the hell does that mean?" I said, getting more annoyed with every statement she made.

"Remember when Britney had her babies, and the world thought she was so over? And then suddenly she started showing up with Paris Hilton at nightclubs and forgetting to wear her panties? That was all just PR—she wanted to be the bad girl again because everyone just saw her as a mom, and there is nothing more deadly boring than being a mom."

"Oh, really? I thought she just forgot them," I huffed as I rolled my eyes. "I'm not an idiot, Dev. I understand how the celebrity game works. I mean, I read *US Weekly*."

"But that's just it," she said. "We're playing the same game at old Millbank High. It's just in a really, really small pond."

She paused for a second to gather her thoughts, and for some reason I kept seeing my super-popular, wonder-woman of a sister shaking her head at me and saying, "Kate, you'll never be that girl. . . ." Even with her away at college, I was still haunted by her popularity.

"But it's more than just PR," Dev continued. "That's only part of running a business."

"A business," I said deadpan.

"Sure. They're treating you like a commodity, so why not act like one? C'mon, I'm great at business stuff. We can totally transform you."

Her confidence made it seem so easy, like if I just followed her plan—whatever it was—I could go from nobody to somebody in a couple of weeks. It couldn't be that easy, I thought, or everyone would do it.

"I've studied these girls," she continued, as her tone changed—a sadness inflecting her voice. "Do you think I just pulled this all out of a hat? Are you that blind? I've been trying to think of a way to go from 'mouse' to 'maven' for four years. And while I see the right steps, I can't do it, but *you* can."

I was dumbfounded. Dev had just confessed to me her innermost anxieties and fears, albeit in a rather odd way. She wanted to be this so-called Latebloomer—I mean, I guess we all do—and that's why she knew about these girls already. Dev was like every one of us; she wanted to be somebody. Even with all her brains and the protection they granted her, she was as desperate and as vulnerable as the rest of us. I suddenly felt ashamed for not recognizing the obvious before me, for not recognizing how badly she wanted to be somebody other than who she was.

"But why me?" I questioned, staring down.

"First, you're beautiful, and you don't even know it.

You're intelligent and have just enough artistic brilliance that you can imagine a new you. To become *that* girl, you have to imagine yourself as *that* girl."

I just sat there. The whole idea sounded like science fiction, but then I thought about being Number Seventy-one and how awful that had made me feel. I thought of Will and how much I wanted him to want me. And I thought of Gretchen and how wonderful it would be to knock her off her pedestal. But most of all I could imagine in my mind's eye my mother telling my sister how popular her little sister had become, more popular than she had ever been.

"What about the money—I don't have five hundred dollars to blow on a lottery ticket," I said.

"A Megabucks lottery ticket is about one hundred forty-eight million to one," she said. "Given that you're already Seventy-one—our odds are a helluva lot better. I'm willing to make that bet."

"I'm lost here."

"I'll front it," she said. "If we win, I'll split it with you and Callie."

"Callie?" I said.

She looked me up and down, and then smiled. "Oh yeah, we can't do this alone. You need an intervention!"

BOOK TWO

. . . .

PENNY STOCK

BUSINESS PLAN FOR KATE WINTHROP
Formulated by Devlin Rayner

OBJECTIVE:

To take Kate Winthrop from junk bond on The Millbank Social Stock Market to a Blue Chip in the next four weeks.

COMPETITIVE ANALYSIS:

Your competitors in the Market are girls we already know well: Gretchen Tanner, Elisa Estrada, Jodi Letz, etc. But rather than worrying about their stock, we're simply going to focus on taking your stock from good . . . to great!

DEVELOPMENT PLAN & MILESTONES:

1. **Reinvent the Brand**—bottom line, Kate, you need a major makeover. This is Business 101. Hair, nails, clothes . . . everything (sorry, but it's true!). We have to have an improved product to sell.

2. **The Big Bang Theory**—we will introduce the new you in an explosive way that blows everyone away. You can't just walk into school and hope somebody notices you. We have to create an EVENT to launch your brand.

3. **Establish Brand Loyalty**—to be honest, I haven't quite figured this one out yet (maybe you could bake free cupcakes? offer people rides to school?), but the goal is to get everyone to want to be part of your life.

4. **Co-Branding**—often by associating yourself with another super-successful brand, you can capture some of its heat and improve your own business. Just look at big partnerships—Nike and Tiger Woods, Beyoncé and L'Oréal . . . Nick Lachey and Jessica Simpson (sure, it didn't work out, but hey, look what it did for their careers!). Who can we co-brand with? Will B.? The Proud Crowd? An unknown mystery man?

5. **Paradigm Shift**—just when people think they have a handle on what you are, you will reposition yourself in a new radical act. Bottom line: a little act of rebellion.

6. **Merger & Acquisition**—this is a big one. Often an upstart business needs to merge with a competitor, or . . . if it has enough cash flow . . . acquire it (i.e., AOL and Time Warner, Paramount and DreamWorks). In your case, you're going to co-opt the biggest brand there is at Millbank: Gretchen Tanner.

*****Intangible Alchemy**—now, this isn't exactly a business term, but in business—like life—you need a little good, old-fashioned luck. Hopefully, there'll be some moment that allows the other six steps to come together in a way that's more than simply the sum of the parts. You can't plan this one—you can only prepare for it; and then strike!

CHAPTER

8

THE REST OF the week passed while Dev finished what she called her "business plan." I was a little surprised by how seriously she was taking this—did we really need a big proposal?—but it was classic Dev: methodical, precise, and fixated. While I waited for the saga to begin, with each day I found myself getting more excited. Could we really do what Dev claimed? Could I bail myself out from the social dregs of Millbank High and suddenly become an It Girl? Could I actually be more popular than my sister ever was? To be totally honest, I wasn't so sure. But the way I saw it, what was the worst thing that could happen? If I didn't move at all, and I stayed there stuck at seventy-one, no one would even notice.

So why not give it a shot?

On Friday night, Dev picked me up and drove me over to Callie's house for our "board meeting" all-nighter. On the way, she dropped the bomb on me.

"Okay. Here it is."

"What?"

She reached into her bag, pulled out a leather folder, and removed a sheaf of papers. "Here's what we'll cover for our first board meeting."

I snatched it from her hands and scanned the pages. It was elaborate, to say the least, and I was only able to make it through the first page. Basically, it was made up of seven steps, and most of them didn't make a whole lot of sense to me. It was a lot of business jargon, but the first step a two-year-old could've understood. *Makeover.* Dev's term for it was "reinvent the brand," but I understood what it really meant.

"What's wrong with how I am now?" I asked.

"I just know the necessary steps," Dev answered. "I leave the analysis and judgment to the experts. Let's see what Callie has to say."

Earlier in the week, she had called Callie to rope her in on what she had jokingly titled Project Re-eduKate. While Dev may have been a genius with business and computers, she was hardly a fashion plate, so she called Callie and told her about our plan for total transformation. Callie's sense of style was a wild mix: part fashionista, part rock star, all amazing. But when Dev explained everything to Callie and asked for her help, there was just silence at the other end of the speaker phone.

"Are you kidding me?" she answered. "Not a chance."

We were speechless. I looked at Dev, and she raised hands as if to say, "I have no idea what she's all worked up about." Dev had already e-mailed her the link to the MSSM, and while Callie reveled briefly in her own status as Number Eleven, she was very down on the idea of playing the market, so to speak.

"Don't you realize how offensive this game is to women?" she began. "It's classic male bull—objectifying women— and assigning values to them. You really want to be part of this?"

"Don't start with that feminist crud," Dev said.

"It isn't feminism—and even if it were, hello, there's nothing wrong with that. It's just common sense, which the two of you have apparently lost."

There was a long pause on the phone while none of us said anything.

"You two think playing the popularity game is fun," Callie said finally. "But trust me—it's an obsession like any other. And it'll ruin you and your friendship. So I'm out."

With that, she hung up, and Dev and I stared at each other, apparently thwarted at the very beginning of our journey.

But fifteen minutes later, right when Dev and I were

combing through the *Teen Vogue* Web site, pathetically searching for fashion ideas, Callie called back.

"All right. I'm in," she sulked. "But only because I love you and want you to look good. But don't come crying to me when it's all over."

Dev and I arrived at her house still squabbling over my fashion sense. Callie was sitting in her kitchen with a mug of chamomile tea, sporting a T-shirt that read, ORDINARY.

I laughed when I saw it, knowing how ironic it truly was.

"Ladies," she said with a grin, "welcome to the fashion dome."

Dev sat next to Callie, and they pointed to an uncomfortable chair that had been conspicuously placed across the room.

Was this a makeover or an inquisition?

"Why are we here, Kate?" Callie asked. She started tapping her pencil against a sketch pad on her lap.

"Ummm . . . because I need a makeover," I said. "But can I just say first that I think I have a pretty good style all my own? I'm pretty cool, right?"

Hello, it's true. Sure, I wasn't fabulous like Callie, but my cute little jean-jacket thing worked okay.

Apparently Callie and Dev didn't agree. They exchanged a look.

"I told you," Dev said low to Callie.

Told her what?

"Kate, you know how much I love you, right?" Callie said, as she turned back to me. "Then I'm only going to tell you this out of love and because there's no time to waste. You're a fashion *disaster*."

I'm so going to live to regret all this.

"And to make things worse, you suffer from what I like to call schizo-fashion-phrenia. It's a disease, and it affects young girls who think putting on the right color top to go with a jean jacket is 'a look.'"

"Harsh," Dev said. "But oh so true."

Callie turned and pursed her lips.

"If I were *you*," she said, looking at Dev, "I'd reserve any commentary you may have, because you're just as bad with your smart-girl glasses and your half-goth-half-just-pasty-because-you-don't-get-enough-sun look."

Dev cowered into her chair and zipped it. I tried to suppress the smile that crept across my face. It felt good to have somebody else's fashion sense destroyed in a single sentence.

"Okay, fine. Maybe I could try harder," I relented. "But I do have a style all my own."

"What's your style, Kate?" Callie said, putting up her hand. "When in doubt, throw on J. Crew and look like everybody else? You know what I call that? Mutt Fashion. Do you know what a mutt is?"

Did I look like an idiot *and* a fashion disaster?

"It's a dog," she continued. "Occasionally cute like you, but defined mostly by its lack of definition. It isn't a collie or Lab or dachshund. It's a little bit of everything, but it adds up to a whole lot of nothing."

By now I'm sure I must've looked pretty shell-shocked, because Callie took it down a notch.

"I'm sorry, honey. Dev told me this was a fashion intervention, so I'm laying it on a bit thick. Believe me, you've got everything you need, you just need to put it together the right way. The hair, the nails, and then clothes—we'll make it work for you. But you have to have faith. Are you with me?"

"I guess so, but can I keep my jean jacket?" I said.

She put her finger to her lips. "Hush, little girl. You don't need your safety blanket anymore," she said. "You're in my hands now."

Millbank isn't known as the fashion capital of the world, but it has a few good spots, so come Saturday morning we decided to stay local. Callie said she wanted to avoid what she called the obvious styles and create something new and bold for me.

"You can't shop at the mall," she said. "That's for the common herd only."

We were walking toward a vintage shop called Lucky's.

It was on North Adams just after it crosses River Road, by the Ice Cream Palace. We'd ditched Dev, who had to go home and do some research and development (or "R&D" in business lingo) for our other six steps.

"There are two types of people, Kate: sheep and wolves," Callie mused. "Sheep wait to see what everybody else is wearing, and then they run out to the mall and buy it. That's fine if you want to blend in. But wolves eat sheep."

"What are you?" I asked, thinking I was being coy. "Sheep or wolf?"

"Me," Callie mused. "I eat wolves."

Okay. This girl, a girl whom I'd been best friends with for eons, was starting to scare me.

We walked into Lucky's, and while Callie looked through the racks, I checked myself out in a mirror. Was she really right about my look? I'd worn this jean jacket with some form of J. Crew wear for three years now. Had I really been that blind? I realized that there was nothing wrong with it per se, but there was nothing special there either. If you put a paper bag over my head, I probably could've been any one of a hundred girls in the halls of Millbank High School.

"All right," Callie shouted from across the room. "Come check this out."

She was holding a very old Lacoste shirt, bright green, circa 1986. I'm pretty sure the color is chartreuse, and it was probably two sizes two small. She started rifling through the racks and tossing clothes into a basket. Short shorts. A vintage von Furstenberg wrap dress. An old GUNS N' ROSES T-shirt. A blue blazer. A pleated skirt like Catholic school girls wear. Cut-off denim shorts.

"What's all this?"

"The new Kate," she said. "And FYI, let's change your name while were at it. We're going to call you Kat, like a sexy, smart little kitten." She giggled like she'd hit upon something clever.

I wasn't sure about the whole name thing or the clothes, and frankly, I couldn't make sense of them either. In some ways they were within the realm of what I was wearing already, but they were pure vintage, and tighter and sexier, to boot. As Callie's vision started to jell in my mind, I started imagining outfits I could put together, and I wasn't entirely sure that my mother wouldn't have a complete and total heart attack.

"You're going for prep," I said cautiously. "But . . ."

"But sexy prep. Lacoste with a drop of Paris," she explained. "The tart, not the city."

"Right," I replied. "Not more than a drop or two, though—I mean, she's a skank."

Callie laughed. "Indeed. A skank who's worshipped because she was an original, although a skanky original."

We both cracked up.

"By the time I'm done"—she grinned—"nobody's even going to recognize you."

Four hours later, Dev joined us and we were all sitting in Images, waiting for Carlo. I was halfway done with my makeover, and a new hair style was part two. My new wardrobe—although mostly thrift store—had ended up costing some serious change, but Dev had offered to front most of the cost. What can I tell you? It's pretty helpful to have friends with gobs of money when you're doing a total makeover, and Dev was generous like that.

Now that I was face-to-face with actually going forward with this insane plan, however—i.e. cutting, straightening, and dyeing my hair—I was more than a little hesitant.

Clothes you could always throw away.

A new hairstyle was permanent.

I looked at Dev. "Remind me why I'm doing this again?"

"Because of the Market?" she said, looking less than convinced by her own rhetoric.

"There has to be some other reason. Am I really that shallow?" I said.

"You're so beautiful, Kat," Callie piped in. "You are just showing the world what I've known—that you are a star. There's nothing wrong with shining."

But what was my mother going to say when I got home, and it looked like a diva had commandeered the body of her hitherto super-conventional daughter? On the other hand, I *did* like the way I looked in the new clothes that Callie had found for me. A little older, a little more daring, a little over the edge. For the first time, I felt like I'd been given permission to show a little more leg, let loose, and nudge a little closer to a wilder side. But truth be told, I still wasn't sure I was ready to make that leap.

"Katie," Carlo called in his thick Peruvian accent as he approached, "Devie here tells me you want to be wild. Tell me it's true."

I looked skeptically at Dev, who made a face that said, "Don't disappoint Carlo." I turned to him and laid some puppy-dog eyes on him.

"I'm not sure."

"You are not sure about what?" he quizzed. In a whirl he ushered me to a chair, and before I could answer, he'd already spritzed my hair with water and was gently massaging my scalp.

Carlo was flamboyant, gay, and a force with which to be reckoned. We all loved how over-the-top he was. He'd moved to Millbank from the West Village about five years ago and quickly became the rage among the under-twenty crowd. There was a little boutique salon around the corner, but that was for the rich and the old (with kids). Images and Carlo, they were for the hip and the young. No toddlers allowed.

"Let me tell you, Katie, the truth about women," he started in.

And this was the other thing about Carlo: he loved to hear himself talk. Once he got started, there was no stopping him. He was the king of pontification; you give him a subject, he had an opinion. I would say he was right only fifty percent of the time, but he was so damn sure of himself, you just couldn't help but listen.

"Every day," he continued, "women come to Carlo and ninety-nine out of a hundred stay just like before. *Boring.* But once a month there's a woman who says, 'Carlo, I want to be a star . . . Carlo, make me a star,' they say. And you know what?"

"What?"

"Carlo does!"

"Maybe I don't want to be a star."

"No!" Carlo shouted. "*Everyone* wants to be a star."

I closed my eyes. So the moment of decision was truly at hand.

I could hear Callie and Dev mmm-hmming and nodding, but I didn't say a word. I opened my eyes and looked into the mirror in front of me. I'd always wondered what life would be like as a blonde. Did they really have more fun? I looked at the clothes I was wearing, the old jean jacket and the maroon L.L. Bean button-down.

Was Callie right? Was this jacket my blankie? Did I carry

around this piece of cloth because it made me feel safe? Was Carlo right? Was my fear holding me back from what I truly wanted?

In a flash I stood up. I could see Callie and Dev were nervous, thinking I was about to walk out, but instead I whipped off my jean jacket and tossed it to Dev.

"Take this and hide it till school is over. Callie, could you shorten those skirts we bought just a bit—a little more leg? And Carlo, I want to go blond. And make it as sexy as you can."

"Whooooo-HOOOOO!" is all I heard from the three of them.

Carlo did a little mambo—or some South American dance—and then took out the coloring bottles and asked me to choose which color blond I wanted to be. Misty Dawn? Honey Blond? Corn Straw? I never realized there were so many choices.

Callie pulled out the plaid skirt and held it up. "Now, how short do you want this?" she asked.

"Where the mystery begins," I replied.

Dev and Callie nearly fell on the floor with laughter.

"Where did you hear that line?" Dev asked after she composed herself.

I shrugged, smiling. I had no idea where it came from, but I made a note to ramp it down. I was quickly realizing that once you let your inner Paris out, it was hard to keep her in check.

Three and a half hours later, I was within a single shade of platinum blond. Yeah, I'd gone all out. And maybe, just maybe, I'd gone a little too far. But as any girl knows, when you sit for two and a half hours watching the "paint" dry on your hair, you have more than a little time to contemplate life's big questions. Looking in the mirror and watching my curly brown hair turn straight and blond, I found the question of why I was doing this impossible to avoid.

I thought of Mom and Mel's close relationship and how desperately I wanted to be part of what they had; of always being the six or seventh or whatever number picked for anything (never the first and never the last, which I always thought must have had its own charms); of never being the "-est" girl in anything, and by that I mean never the pretty-est, smart-est, sexy-est, tall-est, fast-est. Every one of us, old or young, smart or dumb, ugly or beautiful, wants to be somebody. It's why people read *Us Weekly* and think they are reading about friends. It's why in England people follow the trials and tribulations of British royalty. We all have a never-ending thirst to be more "important" than we are. "I want to be somebody," I felt like shouting over the hum of hair dryers and electric buzz cutters. I wanted everyone to know me, to remember me, to be on the lips of strangers who told stories about me like they knew me . . . as if I were their friend. If changing my hair, coloring it blond, and jet-tisoning every piece of clothing that screamed of the old, invisible me was what I needed to do, then I was more than willing to do it.

When Carlo removed the towel from my head, blew out my hair, and I saw the new me, I was sure I'd made the right move.

I got up from my chair and, at the prompting of Callie, did a short catwalk for the girls. Carlo and the girls applauded, and Stephania (Carlo's station mate) gave me the thumbs-up. Yup, this was going to be the start of a whole new life.

The life of Kat.

But when I turned around and started walking back toward the chair, I stopped dead in my tracks. It wasn't the new me in the mirror, or the ghost of the old me standing there in disbelief. No, it was worse.

It was my mother—and her jaw was on the floor.

I'd forgotten that the third Saturday of every month was re-coloring day. She liked coming to Images, she said, because it made her feel young. (Hey, moms, that makes the rest of us feel old!) With her hands gripping a swivel chair she'd apparently grabbed to prevent her from fainting, she looked like she was about to kill somebody. Me. Carlo. Callie. Dev. I'm not exactly sure who, but she had murder in her eyes. Callie and Dev—veterans of my mother's anger— wilted like two week-old flowers and grabbed their stuff before bolting for the door. Dev gave me the "Call me" sign, and Callie shrunk her six-foot frame and skittered out like a mouse. I nodded to them and then slinked back into Carlo's chair, hoping for some protection, but he just raised his eyebrows nervously and straightened up his station.

My mother strode up to me and spun the chair around. She stood there for what felt like an eternity.

"Hey, Mom," I said.

When in serious trouble, pretend nothing is wrong.

"What were you thinking?" she hissed.

Yes, there's nothing quite like a parent to rain on your parade.

"I'd like an answer. Now!"

I was silent. I mean, I couldn't tell her the truth. What? That there was a list going around school and that I was on the bottom of it? That only would've confirmed all her criticism over the years.

"I wanted to do something special," I replied. "Something different."

"Different? Different?" she stammered. "Different is ironing your sweater for a change. Not deciding you want to look like Suzanne Somers."

I looked at Carlo and said, "Who?" He put his hands up and made an I-don't-know-either face.

"I think she looks beautiful," Carlo chimed.

My mother gave him the evil eye, and he shuffled to the other side of the room.

"Let's go."

I gathered my bags and gave a hidden wave to Carlo, who blew me a kiss. Right when I reached the door, he motioned subtly and mouthed something to me. At first I didn't get it, but when he said it the second time, I couldn't help but smile.

"You're a star."

CHAPTER

```
........
: 9 :
........
```

ON ALMOST ANY other night in my high school career, you'd have found me studying, but as graduation loomed ever closer, I relaxed. I'd already been accepted to Brown and I knew I could coast to the end without seriously jeopardizing my grades. Most teachers understood the need to kick back a little as we approached June, so allowances were made and grades were inflated. It was a little game we all consciously took part in, but of which we never spoke.

So there I was, supine on the sofa in the basement. TNT had a teen movie marathon and I was watching *Can't Buy Me Love*—a classic—with Remington curled on the pillow at my feet. Upstairs, my parents were hanging out, no doubt discussing what had happened to their curly-brown-haired daughter. The ride home from Images with Mom was oh-so-pleasant—she laid into me for a good fifteen minutes about the damage I'd done to my hair between the dye and the straightening, and demanded to know if I was on drugs. Yeah, she was a little prone to hysterics. Silently I figured that she was actually just freaked because the interview for the Millbank Country Club was coming up, and she was worried how it would seem to the committee if her daughter looked like Christina Aguilera in her glam days, but I didn't call her on it. I've found over time that it's best just to let parents blow all their steam out, and then respond later. Engaging them in their moments of rage only stokes the fire.

As the show went to commercial break, I heard the buzz of my cell phone and my first thought was to just ignore it. Then the ridiculous thought that perhaps Will B. might be calling—hey, we all like to fantasize—literally pulled me right off the couch. When I glanced at the caller ID, I sighed.

"Hey, Cal," I said.

"What are you doing right now?" she asked.

There was an urgency in her voice, like the world was about to come to an end.

"Lying down and dreaming about McDreamy," I answered.

"Well, wake up and start dreaming about boys your own age," she shouted. "Meet me at the Café Electric at ten p.m."

"I already told my parents I was staying in for the night. You know how they are."

What I didn't bother adding was that my mother was probably still really pissed at me and that it was best to let sleeping dogs lie.

"Did you forget that Will B. and his band are playing at open mike, and everybody who's anybody is going to be there? So you've got to get there, too. It's time to introduce Kat to the world."

I said nothing. Truth is, the thought of trotting out the new me was terrifying. Prancing around in front of Carlo and my friends was one thing, but out in public? That was altogether different. What if everyone thought I looked ridiculous? What if everyone laughed? What if this whole transformation thing had been a big mistake?

"I don't know," I hedged.

"Sheep or wolf?" Callie shot back. "Do you want to explode like the big bang or whimper like a mutt in the rain?"

Dev had obviously gotten into her brain, too.

"Okay," I said, without thinking. "I'll meet you out front."

"By the Cuban place," she said.

I hung up and ran to my room. I dug through all my new outfits and considered what would be best for the occasion. I pulled out a little white pleated skirt Callie had picked out and a sexy yoga tank that made me look more full-figured than I really was, but that was the point, after all. My hair was still perfect—maybe a little flat in the back from lying on the sofa—but there was no need to fuss with it. I grabbed the highest heels I could walk in, the little Kate Spade bag Callie had loaned me, and threw in my keys and a couple of twenties.

But as I reached for the door, it hit me: if I walked out into my living room dressed like this, my parents would flip. Like Superman—or Supergirl, I suppose—I quickly undressed and threw everything into a little gym bag, including my purse. Instead, I put on an old ratty pair of jeans, flip-flops, and my Mack Trucks baseball cap.

Now there are any number of excuses you can give your parents when you're trying to get out of the house, but here's the problem: almost none of them work. If it were my dad, I'd probably have used the tried-and-true "I'm going to get tampons." With Mom sitting there, however, that was out the window, so I opted for the classic intimate-talk trick.

"Mom, could I talk to you for a minute, *alone?*" I whispered from the doorway.

Adding the "alone" part is key. We moved to the kitchen, where I lied and explained that Dev had just been dumped by a boy she hardly knew but was hoping might ask her to the Black & White (note how I played on my mother's own anxiety about me—the Black & White and that damn club?). While things weren't exactly hunky-dory between us since the whole Images drama, she nodded as if she understood and told me to call if I was going to be late or sleeping over.

Flawless.

I was out the door and in my car in a matter of seconds. I had to get re-dressed, but the question was, where? The passenger seat of my incredibly glamorous 1996 two-door Honda Civic was far from spacious, and Millbank wasn't one of those rural towns with lots of empty spaces where you could ditch your car in the woods and feel pretty safe that nobody was going to come along and see you. So I pulled into the community parking lot and drove to the very top, where there were no cars, and parked in the darkness of a corner spot. It took me a few minutes to wrangle out of my jeans into my skirt, but like Superman in a phone booth, when I emerged, I was ready to fly.

River Road was always hopping (at least by suburban standards), but tonight it seemed especially busy. There were probably twenty restaurants on the main drag and more than a handful of bars. People from all over the area came to Millbank to party, some to see hip indie films, some to get a bite at restaurants like Violet or Lex that served New York–quality food in New Jersey. The media-savvy citizens of Millbank, many of them in the "biz" (as they like to refer to anything entertainment-related), thought of their little town as the "sixth" borough. Others, less generous, liked to call it the Upper West Side of New Jersey. I, like any other American kid, called it home . . . and I couldn't wait to get as far away as possible.

As I walked down River, in the distance I could see Callie standing in front of Café Electric, playing with her big hoop earrings. She looked cool in wide-wale cords and her purple Crocs, but it was hardly the outfit for a night at Café Electric.

Why would she wear that?

"Hey, Cal." I waved and gave her a light look up and down, as if to say, "Really?"

"You look delicious, Kat. I could eat you up."

"Thanks," I said. I glanced down at my heels, saw a trace of mud that I whisked off with my pinky finger.

"Here's the plan," she whispered into my ear. "I'll hang out here. You go in and do your stuff."

"What?" I snapped. "I'm not going in by myself."

For starters, I'd never been in Café Electric in my life. Second, I was supposed to roll in there, sporting a whole new wardrobe, a whole new hairstyle, without a wing girl? I shook my head again, but Callie smiled her comforting, wide grin. She put her arm around my shoulder and walked me to the alley beside Electric.

96

"Listen up," she said calmly. "You need to go in there and be bigger than life. If I'm there—well—that's going to be tough. We'll end up sucking each other's energy right out of the room."

"No way."

First Gretchen's party, now Café Electric. Since when did I have to face the world alone?

"So it's the same old Katie, but with different clothes," Callie sighed. "I get it."

I could see the remarks on the Market already: "Looks like someone dropped a bottle of peroxide on her head!" or "Fashion Disaster 101" or "Who would've thought that she could look lamer than before?" But whatever, I thought. If I didn't do it, it would probably read: "Didn't see her out; must have stayed home with cats on Saturday night."

"Fine, tell me what I have to do."

I walked to the door of Electric and paid the ten-dollar cover charge to see the open-mikers. Pushing my way through the crowd, I made my way down the hall to the back of the club where the stage was, and as soon as I set foot in the room, I felt my body tense up. Millbank students packed the place, and nearly every table was taken. Callie was right— anyone who was anyone was here. In the very back in the corner—no doubt weaving her black widow's web—was Gretchen surrounded by the Proud Crowd posse. There were others I knew—some seniors, some recent grads who went to nearby colleges—but Callie had given me very specific instructions: I wasn't allowed to talk to anyone I knew. There was no safety in familiarity. I was to be bold. I was supposed to walk right to the edge of the stage, sit down, and just stare into Will's eyes as he sang. Callie's theory was that if Will noticed me, everyone else would notice me, hence launching my new look—or "brand" as Dev would say— into the stratosphere. That's the big bang model, anyway.

In theory? Easy.

In reality? Terrifying.

Let's all remember that exactly one week ago I was the girl wandering around Gretchen's party unable to work the tap at the keg.

Well, that doesn't matter now, I reminded myself. I checked the mirrored wall across the room to see if there was any trace of the little girl who was frightened of everything, of everyone, and for the first time . . . I didn't see her. Not totally, at least. Maybe I didn't see Kat either, but I saw somebody different, striving however awkwardly to be something else.

I took a deep breath, held my head high, and took my first step across the room.

I was going to do it. It was time to show the world the new me.

Say hello to Kat!

And right then, the whole mirage came crashing down around me.

My right heel slipped on something—a wet napkin . . . a crack in the floor?—and for a pregnant moment that seemed like forever, I felt myself falling sideways. It's safe to say that "graceful" has never been an adjective used to describe me, and images of me eating it into a table—cups of soda and coffee drenching my new outfit, and people hysterically laughing over me as I lay on the floor, perhaps even bleeding from a fresh gash in my forehead—flashed through my mind like a bad movie. This was it. Just when I thought I might be making my jump to super cool, I was about to become super loser!

But in an instant—and with agility I'd never realized I had—I threw my right hand out onto an empty chair and miraculously caught my balance. I shot a quick look around, and—thank God!—I could tell nobody noticed. Adjusting myself once more, I shook it off and began taking long catwalk-like strides across the room. I kept my eyes focused on a spot in the distance, and zeroed in on an empty chair.

Don't fall, Kate.

Please, please, please don't fall.

And as I walked down the center aisle toward the stage, praying that I wasn't going to make a total ass of myself, the strangest thing happened. I could see the shadows of boys' heads turn my way and the heavy eyes of girls fall upon me.

As I passed tables, a hush trailed behind me. I glanced back once, just to make sure that it wasn't Gretchen making the room stand still. And it wasn't.

It was me.

I was making it happen!

I sat down at the first table just to the left of the stage, but—and forgive the cliché—I was floating on air. The whole thing had been so intoxicating—almost how I imagined the strongest of drugs. In the wings, I spotted Will B. working with his drummer, Dee Brown, trying to get his kit ready for their song. A waiter strolled up, gave me a wink, and took my order. (I could get used to this!)

After a few minutes the lights dimmed and Jane Austen's Secret Lover was introduced. The band came out led by Jack, who tuned his guitar and strummed a few notes. After a moment of settling, Will B. stalked to the middle of the stage and straddled the microphone stand. It was like a slow dance with a girl he loved. Jack started a hard guitar riff—intently focusing down—and gradually the music began to build, like the best of The Shins or the Yeah Yeah Yeahs. About two thirds of the way through their song, while the drummer ripped off a solo, Will came out of his performance-inspired coma and looked around, searching the crowd, it seemed, for familiar faces. Suddenly, his eyes met mine, and I gave my gaze all the intensity I could muster.

But nothing happened. His eyes fell away as if I weren't there.

For a moment I felt crestfallen—crushed is probably the better word—but then, like an electromagnet whose power is delayed, he came back to me with a fierce look, and howled a few more bars. I kept my cool, but I knew for whom he was singing. Me!! My stomach flip-flopped around and my legs wobbled, but on the outside, I'm pretty sure I kept my cool.

As the mini-set ended, I checked my watch; it was three minutes before midnight. Deep down, I hoped that Will would come and talk to me—perhaps he was wondering who the blonde in the front row was—but I was going to leave at twelve. This was the last thing Callie had told me. As soon as midnight rolled around, no matter what was happening, I was supposed to get up and walk out.

"Arrive late, leave early," she'd advised.

A few moments later, Will and Jack and the rest of the band disappeared behind the stage, and I was sure that would be the last I'd see of him. I went to grab my purse from the table, but an instant later he entered the room from the EMPLOYEES ONLY door on the opposite side. Will sauntered right up to my table with Jack in tow, and I could swear he gave a soft wave to Gretchen as if to say, "What up." What I definitely saw was her sit back in disgust.

"Kate!" He grinned. "You look awesome."

"Thanks," I said. "You were wonderful. You too, Jack." Jack gave me a little nod and then continued to stare at the ground. Just then, Dee Brown—the drummer and a boy I had known since fifth grade—bounced up and introduced himself.

"Hey, I'm Dee."

"Dude, don't be an idiot," Will said, hitting him playfully. "It's Kate Winthrop."

Dee's mouth fell open ever so slightly in disbelief. "Holy acts of total makeover."

Will grabbed a chair and swung it around so he was sitting backward on it and leaning over the back in a relaxed, I-don't-care-what-the-world-thinks way. Frankly, I didn't care either. He was the dreamiest thing I'd ever seen.

Jack stood directly behind Will, and he looked up from his shoes and stared at me. His unwavering gaze would have made me feel awkward in any other situation, but my entire focus was easily placed on Will.

"Hey, Will," Jack said. "We need to break down the gear so the next band can set up."

"Sure, sure," Will waved him off, keeping his eyes on me. "I'll be right there."

Jack sighed and headed back toward the stage.

"Are you hanging here?" Will asked.

"Not sure," I said. I looked at my watch and it read midnight on the dot. *Crap.* I gave myself a little more rope and told myself to be out by 12:05 a.m.

"We're getting together at my house," he said.

I nodded and asked who "we" was.

"You know, just some peeps, the usual suspects," he answered.

I nodded again, though I had no idea who he was talking about.

Just then I heard my cell go off and picked it out of my purse. I looked at the caller; it was a text from Callie:

CAL: Leave the glass slipper on the table, princess.

I laughed a little and looked at Will.

"Who's that?" he asked.

"Oh, nobody," I answered, with the coolest of shrugs. With every waking second, I could feel my confidence growing. "But I have to go."

I stood up. In my heels I was a good inch or so taller than Will, and he looked up at me. I could see he was a little starry-eyed, and for the first time in my life, I knew what the word "power" meant.

"Later, Jack," I said as he waved from the stage. Then with a knowing touch on the back of Will's hand, I whispered, "Bye, Will—maybe next time."

KCW LLC.

MARKET RANKING: 59
TODAY'S CHANGE: ↑12

SHARE PRICE: $3.75
CHANGE: ↑1.90 (+102%)
L/B RATIO: 5.3
3-MONTH RANGE: $1.23 – $3.77
STATUS: PENNY STOCK

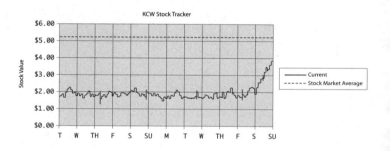

ANALYST RECOMMENDATION: a significant repackaging has this analyst taking a closer look. Tongues were wagging at Café Electric, but it remains to be seen if new management will stay the course and do what needs to be done to truly transform this stock into a buy.

HOLD

CHAPTER

10

WHEN I WOKE UP Sunday morning, I had a hangover. Not from booze, mind you, but from the euphoria of the night before that had settled to the back of my brain and morphed into something new and heavy. There were now two of me living in one body. On one side of the bed, the little girl in the jean jacket—still thinking of herself as the wallflower. Beside her, awakened for the first time by a kiss from destiny, was a radiant young woman who was just opening her eyes and seeing for the first time a big wide world.

Sadly, the old me looked at her clock radio and knew there wasn't even enough time to roll out of bed and get to the BookStop before opening. Thus, a mere sixty seconds later, I was in my standard BookStop uniform: jeans and a Che T-shirt (courtesy of Howie). But as I grabbed my purse and headed for the door, I caught a glimpse of myself in the mirror.

I paused.

Although I'd always thought the look was original, it dawned on me that maybe I just looked like every other little faux radical in Millbank. We wore our T-shirts protesting this or that, or we sported clever shirts formerly owned by real gas-station attendants and thought we were cool. But were we? I looked over at the closet and I knew behind the doors was a new outfit—something original and mind blowing. Whatever lurked there was probably totally inappropriate for the BookStop, but I realized that if I wanted to change myself, I had to go whole hog or else the old me would keep seeping into the picture.

I tossed my purse on the bed and started peeling off my clothes.

It took me a few minutes to put together a somewhat fabulous outfit (it's not as easy as it looks) that wouldn't send Howie into total shock. The BookStop was a left-wing bookstore, after all. So here's what I did: I took that Che T-shirt and did a quick nip and tuck, threw on some hip-hugging, navel-blazing jeans, a pair of wedge-heeled boots, and added some jewelry that conveniently dropped pearls right over old Che's beard. For good measure I tied a cool scarf around my neck, and as I finished getting dressed, I even came up with a name for the look: Sexy Che. I'm sure

Señor Guevara rolled over in his grave, but no doubt he admired my audacity.

Twenty minutes later, I pulled open the door to the BookStop, and Howie was already sitting on his stool perched way above me. He did a double take as I walked in, and made a face somewhere between a smirk and a laugh. I was late, to boot, so I'm sure that added to his general disgust.

"Britney Guevara," he observed. "A clever response to the suffocating pressure of a bourgeois middle-class existence."

I breezed by him with the simple joust, "Fidel, fatigues were so yesterday—it's a new world out there." Whether he was caught without a response or just quietly amused by my barb, he didn't respond.

I walked into the employee room, dropped my stuff, and knocked on Mrs. Sawyer's door. She was doing the books—she didn't believe in Microsoft Excel; she literally did all her accounting by hand—and was talking on the phone to someone she apparently didn't like very much.

I nodded and then picked up a box of stuff she had set aside for the graduation window. *A Short Guide to a Happy Life* by Anna Quindlen was sitting on top, followed by a whole host of other stuff about going to college, how to avoid the Freshman Ten, etc.

"I'm going to work on the window for a bit, if that's okay."

She waved me on, and I took the box and slipped back

out into the store. In the comic book section I noticed two stoner types—both sporting those pathetic white-boy cornrows—thumbing through some of the older issues. As I passed by, one of them, who was distinguishable from the other only by an eyebrow pierce, glanced over and gave me a wink.

"What up, *mamacita?*" he cooed.

Needless to say, this was not the sort of attention I was looking for.

I faked a smile and walked to the front of the store. When I opened the hatch that led to the front window, I was greeted by Jack Clayton's mug—it was unshaven and his eyes were a little bloodshot, like he had been up all night.

"Um, what are you doing?"

He pushed himself up off his hands and knees and brushed the dust off his pants. Clearly, my tone caught him off guard. "Hey, Kate."

"*Kat.*"

"Oh, okay," he said. He was distracted and looking around the bay of the front window.

"What are you doing?" I asked again.

"Howie asked me to clean up the window, before we put in the graduation display."

"That's *my* job," I snapped.

Who did he think he was? New people shelve and stack—I do the creative work. Just because he ran with Will didn't mean he could run roughshod over my turf, even if he'd been told to do so. I turned around to go track down Howie, but as I looked across the store, something caught my eye. It was the stoner guys.

They were stealing some of the comic books.

I motioned to Jack with a wave of my hand and then put my finger to my lips.

"What?" he whispered.

"Look." I gestured with my head. "They're shoving comic books down their pants."

"And you want them to put them back?" he quipped.

Nothing like having a clown by your side in a moment of crisis, I thought. Where was Will when I needed him?

I rolled my eyes. Unfortunately, Howie—the usual enforcer—was nowhere to be seen. What should I do? Call the police? No, these guys would have been long gone by then. Confront them myself? Somehow I couldn't quite imagine that I would make a formidable opponent to either in a confrontation. But ignoring them didn't exactly seem like the right thing to do either. Maybe it was my years of working with Howie that roused my righteous indignation, because a moment later I was striding across the store toward them.

Kids, don't try this at home.

"Wait," I heard Jack whisper-shout from behind me, but it was too late.

I snuck up behind them and tapped the pierced one on

the shoulder. When they turned I realized how big these guys were—my head only came to their shoulders—and how much they stank of booze.

"What's that?" I demanded, pointing at the book-size bulge in his crotch.

"You like it?" the piercer said, throwing up his hands in mock innocence.

"Put them back."

"Take 'em back yourself, Lolita," the other joked.

"I'm going to call the po—"

Before I could finish my sentence, eyebrow pierce took off for the back exit, and when I went to grab the other guy—honestly, I don't know what I was thinking—he shoved me into a shelf of self-help books.

"Help!" I yelled as an avalanche of advice fell on me.

In a flash, Jack jumped out from the front window as the book-lifter tried to bolt through the door. He grabbed the dude by the throat and yanked him off his feet and against the wall. *Wow!* Jack was a good three inches shorter and twenty pounds lighter than this guy, but you wouldn't have guessed it by the way he had him pinned against the wall. For the first time, I noticed the size of Jack's hands and forearms—they were weirdly out of proportion to the rest of his body, which I gathered came from thousands of hours of guitar playing. What would've happened if Jack had to hold him for more than a few seconds, I have no idea, but it didn't matter because Howie walked back into the store with a cup of coffee.

"What up?" he asked in perfect teenage speak.

I pointed to the lump in the front of the guy's trousers.

"Glad to see me, huh?" he drawled, but a split second later his face grew dark and threatening. "The merchandise. Now!"

The stoner dropped five or six comic books on the floor before Howie spun him around and yanked out the guy's wallet. He glanced at the driver's license before tossing it back to him.

"Larry Goff? Tell you what, young man, I won't call the cops on you."

The stoner smiled with relief.

"What's your buddy's name?"

"I don't know."

Wrong answer—definitely the wrong answer. A strange grin bordering on psychotic grew on Howie's face.

"Kate, get the police on the phone. Tell them I have somebody here trying to steal this classic pre-film version of *Hell Boy* worth about two thousand dollars—that's grand larceny."

"Mark Altiere—his name is Mark Altiere."

"Thanks, Larry. I'll be calling your parents, and Mark's. And if you come in here again, I'll just break your hands in the back room—got it?"

Larry's face went white, and then he took off out of the store at a full sprint.

"I can't believe they had them down their pants," Howie said, staring down at the comic books. "Now I'm going to have to get rubber gloves and make new cover protectors."

Howie gathered the comics and walked toward the back. When he was gone, I gave Jack a high five.

"Dude, that was awesome. Where'd you learn that?"

He shrugged his shoulders diffidently.

"Listen," I started, "you want to help on the window?"

"The graduation window?" he asked. "Isn't that your thing?"

"Yeah, but I need help. Mrs. Sawyer is too old to spend a couple of hours stooped in the window, and Howie would find a way to offend the entire population of Millbank."

"No doubt," he said. "I can see the Christmas window now, 'A No-Logo Christmas: How to make your own gifts and bomb the System.'"

Observant lad, I thought. He got Howie and, I could tell, still liked him.

"Okay, then," I said, "I like to start with the theme and then find a new way into it. If you do what everyone else is doing, then nobody will stop and notice."

"It's a noisy world," he said.

How true, I thought.

We ended up working steadily for an hour and cleared the bay window, packed the books into boxes, and swept the floor. We took the portable and temporary window stand and put it in place (in between themed windows and holidays, we always put a rack of the rare classics we owned). We hardly said a word the whole time, but by then I was starting to get a good vibe from Jack. When he liked doing something, like playing guitar or, in this case, taking down the window, he was supremely focused. You could tell by looking at his face that he was serious, more serious than most kids in high school. Considering his scene at Millbank, I expected something far different, and part of me wondered if he didn't hang with the Proud Crowd more from circumstance than want. As the day wound down, we traded a few ideas about what the window should be, but none were really sparking.

"Why don't we put this on ice?" he said eventually.

"Really? Graduation's like a month from now."

"I think better when eating. How 'bout we hit Dickey Dogs on Saturday? You in?"

Was Jack asking me out on a date? Two weeks before I would've been over the moon to be asked out by him, but for some reason, I hesitated. Was it because I was hoping Will might ask me out, too? Then, a much tougher calculus problem flashed into my mind: what would going out with Jack mean in terms of the Market? Would it have an impact on Will being interested in me—assuming he might be? In about a millisecond, I computed all the possibilities and concluded that in the end it could only be a positive. In the school's eyes it would definitely be perceived as a big step up for me—easily done after dwelling in Anonymityville for four years—and would certainly give me a bounce in my numbers.

"In," I declared. "I'll meet you here."

And as soon as I said it, something warmed in my heart.

BOOK THREE

ON THE BIG BOARD

CHAPTER

11

WEARING MY NEW clothes to Café Electric was one thing.

Wearing them to school was another.

Sure, I was starting to feel more confident—especially with my Market ranking on the rise—but it was still a bit of an adjustment. When I wore my Catholic schoolgirl outfit—with extra short skirt courtesy of Callie—more than a few disapproving eyebrows were raised by teachers I'd known since I was a freshman, but it was all worth it when I noticed later that week that at least two underclassmen had copied my look. How cool is that? Even better was that Will actually started to say "hi" to me whenever I passed him in the halls.

Kate Winthrop, previously a nonentity, was suddenly a legitimate presence at Millbank High School.

Despite it all, I still had some reservations about Dev's master plan. Now that I'd had some time to review it in depth, there were a few things I needed to hash out with her. Yes, I wanted to climb the Market, but I wasn't going to do it at all costs—I had my pride. So Wednesday after school, Dev, Callie, and I called our second "board meeting"—it was sort of ridiculous calling it a board meeting considering it was just the *three* of us, but it was entertaining all the same—and we met up at Bella's, our stalwart pizzeria where Callie worked three days a week.

We sat in the back room and Dev ordered our favorite, the mushroom ravioli *ala famiglia*, with a grande green salad. As we settled in and sipped our waters and devoured old man Giovachinni's fresh bread, Dev took out her business plan.

"So steps one and two have been a success. We've rebranded you and then created a big bang at Café Electric."

"What's next?" Callie said.

She flipped to a page with the words Step Three written in large block letters.

"A month before Kathy Parker went big in '04, she had a car accident. The doctors thought she might be brain-dead, but miraculously, she recovered. Shortly after she returned to school, Eric Benson asked her out. And the rest, as they say, was history."

"And?" I asked, waiting for the punch line.

"Remember I was struggling with a way to establish brand loyalty? Well here's my plan. Read." I swung her notebook around and scanned a paragraph written in Dev's Unibomber-like script.

If she wasn't my best friend and partner in crime, I would have turned her in right there. I pushed the notebook over to Callie, who read it quickly.

"It's pure insanity," I said. "And the answer is N-O."

"You've lost your mind, Dev," Callie seconded.

"What's wrong with faking a car accident?" she asked without an ounce of irony. "We'll bang my car into a tree out by the estate section and nobody will be the wiser! It's the perfect way to get people emotionally invested in you."

She's lost it. Completely and totally.

"I've got a better idea," Callie replied. "We'll cut off her left hand with my dad's power saw—that'll create sympathy . . . and who needs two hands anyway?"

I guess Dev started to see the light, because she spat out her food as she convulsed into laughter.

"No, wait," I countered. "Let's cut off both my arms—then I can be the girl in that documentary who had to do everything with her feet."

"Don't laugh—I actually considered that!" Dev shouted.

I know, I know. Laughing at disabilities is horrible—and, yes, we're going to go straight to hell—but at that moment, it was the most hilarious thing we'd ever heard.

"Okay, that's fair," Dev conceded. "Let's table Number Three for now—I mean, we'll come up with something else, right?"

Callie and I nodded, and Callie scanned the rest of the steps.

"So you think this will work?" Callie asked.

"I've never been more convinced of something in my life," Dev replied with a devilish grin on her face. "Every girl we looked at in those yearbooks last week took one, two, or even three of these steps during her senior year. I'm not saying they did it consciously, but they took them nonetheless. We just have to do them all to cover all the bases."

A bemused look must have shadowed my face because Dev frowned at me. Was she becoming Dr. Frankenstein and I her experimental monster?

"A few steps might be okay," I said. "But seven? People will think I'm a freak."

"I agree," Callie chimed in. "I mean, people might think she's trying too hard. It could backfire in a big way."

"They won't even know," Dev said. "Only we will."

She may have been right, but for the first time, I worried that I might be manipulating people. Manipulating how they felt about me. Sure, no one else would know what we were up to—but *I* would know. Somehow that began to feel bad enough.

"It seems a little wrong, like I'm tricking people

into liking me," I heard myself say.

"Why?" Dev shot back. "People manipulate each other all day long. They wear clothes that supposedly say something about themselves, or they color their hair, or they pretend to like you so you'll help them on a test, or so you'll give them a ride somewhere. Wake up—the whole world is one big sleight of hand," she said. Dev had an edge in her voice, like she was tired of being a victim of that world herself, and this was her chance to strike back.

"But this feels . . . extreme," I countered.

"It *is* extreme," she pressed. "But that Market is even more extreme. If the boys, or the Proud Crowd, or whoever it is, are going to play rough, then we need to play the game rougher. If they're going to judge a book by its cover, then let's give them the hottest damn cover in the world."

She was twisting the old proverb, but I knew she was right on some level. School, life, however you organized it, was one big game, and the only way you were certain to lose was by sitting out. But if you were in, you might as well go all out.

"Cool," I said. "I'll do them all, except Number Three. I don't want sympathy, and I don't want to fake it to get it, even for the Market. I mean, that would make me lower than them, and that's not the point of this. Or is it?"

Dev shook her head and said, "We'll work on the next two, then."

She seemed disappointed, but I'd made a stand, and I felt a little better about things. Could I "co-brand" myself with a cutie like Will B.? Definitely. Could I stand winning that witch Gretchen over? I didn't see it happening in a million years, but I'd certainly give it a shot. And as far as a little rebellion went, well, I hadn't broken a rule in four years, and no one should go through high school without breaking at least one rule, right?

"Okay, then," I said. "Thanks. I really do want to do this, Dev. For all of us, but Number Three is off the table."

She nodded like she understood.

"You saw that nod, right, Callie?" I said.

"Affirmative on the nod."

We all laughed, but as much as I wanted that to come off as a joke, there was a piece of me that was becoming paranoid about Dev's ambitions and how far she was willing to take this little project.

The rest of the night we ate and talked about how to co-opt Gretchen and how dreamy it would be to win over Will . . . even for a day. Briefly we got sidetracked into fantasizing about what we'd do with the money if we won—new cars? a crazy shopping spree?—but Dev steered us back on track and made us focus on how we were going to win. We didn't come up with anything concrete per se, but I felt happier about the whole experiment. For the first time in my life, I felt like I was taking control of the world around me, and all those forces that seemingly worked against me in high school faded away for a few moments. It made me smile, as I drove home, to know I was heading in a direction that, right or wrong, I had chosen.

When I walked in the door, it looked like an Ann Taylor store had exploded in our living room. Half-empty bags littered the floor, and outfits of varying colors and styles were draped over almost every surface. Purses and hats were hung from door handles and the backs of chairs. I would've guessed that Mom was spring cleaning except there were tags on all the clothing.

"Kate, thank God you're home," my mother said as she stood up from behind the sofa. She had a slightly crazed look in her eye and was wearing a dark purple skirt and jacket with a green hat that made her look like an emaciated eggplant.

"Mom, what's going on?"

"Well, I thought I should get a new outfit for our interview at the country club on Friday."

Oh, yeah, our interview.

"So you bought the whole store?"

"It's not the whole store," she chuckled. "I just thought it would be a good idea to have options."

She called it options. I called it mania.

"Besides," she continued, "I'll just return whatever I don't end up wearing."

"As long as you don't make me return it," I laughed.

"And you better not wear one of your 'new' outfits," she said, making exaggerated quotation signs. I took it as an olive branch of sorts.

"Got it . . . they don't wear super-minis at the club."

"Exactly!" She nodded perfunctorily. "So what do you think: pants are more professional, but skirts are more feminine," she noted as she grabbed a floral outfit.

I shrugged my shoulders impotently. "Um . . . do you think it really matters?"

"Of course it matters. Can I show you a few things?"

I should've said no, of course. I should've said I had homework to do. I should've said I had a brain-splitting migraine and that I desperately needed to lie down before my head exploded. But I didn't. Ever trying to be as good as my big sister was . . . I said yes. And so I spent the rest of the evening with my mother, looking at different tops, pants, skirts, blouses, hats, scarves, and combinations—discussing ad nauseam the advantages and disadvantages of each outfit, and whether it was now culturally acceptable to wear white before Memorial Day. We made *Project Runway* look like amateur hour.

By the end, my eyes had glazed over and I silently wondered why my mother was so invested in getting into the club. I mean, who cared? None of her tennis buddies were members, and it wasn't like she needed the pool—we had one in our backyard. Besides, Dad wasn't really into the idea, so why was she?

Thankfully, when my dad arrived home, he put an end to my misery. Seeing my mother in the middle of the living room, surrounded by piles of discarded clothes, with a scarf wrapped around her head like she was Jackie Kennedy, he calmly put down his briefcase and put his hands together in front of his chest.

"Ladies, can I ask a question?"

Mom and I nodded.

"Who are you, and what have you done with my family?"

CHAPTER

12

FRIDAY BROUGHT THE first really warm day of the year, and come lunchtime, most of the senior class was out on the back lawn. Callie, Dev, and I snagged the bench under the old maple and shared a barbecue chicken pizza that Callie had zipped out and picked up from Bella's. Random students lay on the grass around us—heads propped on bags— eager to soak up some rays, while Gretchen and the Proud Crowd were situated around one of the patio tables, apparently sharing the most hilarious joke ever because they couldn't stop laughing. Out by the baseball field, some boys on the Millbank lacrosse team had started an impromptu game of Ultimate, and every now and then an errant Frisbee would land in someone's lunch.

"Did you see our graduation gowns?" Callie asked as

she finished her second slice. "They're hideous. I'm going to talk to Principal Johnson."

We'd all been measured for our gowns earlier that morning, and a sample had hung stiffly behind the disturbingly hairy woman from the company that did the rentals. Callie was right. They *were* hideous. Royal blue, with yellow piping, it was less a graduation gown and more of a carnival outfit. What was wrong with just the standard black?

"Nobody looks good in those things anyway," Dev mumbled as she whipped out her Sidekick. "We'll wear them for three hours and then never see them again."

"Have you *been* to my house?" Callie asked. "My mother already has a spot on the bookshelf for a photo of me at graduation. I'll be seeing that outfit for the rest of my life."

"Maybe you can ask for a close-up," I joked.

It was right then that someone yelled "heads!" before a pink Frisbee whizzed in and nearly decapitated Dev. For once, being short was a plus, because it flew just over her head and ricocheted harmlessly off the tree trunk.

"Watch it!" Callie yelled.

One of the cuter lacrosstitutes broke out from the game and ran toward us. "Sorry 'bout that!"

As the guy neared, he noticed something and his pace slowed. Reaching the Frisbee, he bent over and picked it up.

He didn't leave.

"Hey, Kat," he said with a little lift of his head.

The guy stood there awkwardly waiting for me to respond. Next to me I could feel Callie and Dev look my way, probably wondering the same thing I was.

"Hey," I said, not knowing his name.

"Chris, my name's Chris," he said, as if he could read my mind. (I hoped not, because he was a total hottie!)

"Hey."

"Hey," he replied. A beat later, a couple of his teammates yelled for him to come back. "See ya."

Amused, I smiled and nodded, and he took off.

"Look at you!" Callie giggled. "Just slaying boys left and right."

"I don't know what you're talking about," I managed to reply with a straight face.

"Junior lacrosse players?" Dev said. "C'mon, guys. Big picture. Think Will!"

Granted, Chris Whatever-his-name-was didn't hold a candle to Will, but what was wrong with enjoying a little attention? Or acknowledging that I was in fact becoming more popular?

Suddenly, Dev's Sidekick beeped in her hand, and immediately she checked the message. Grinning, she pumped her fist in the air.

"What?"

"The next step. It's all lined up for three o'clock."

"We're doing a step today?"

She nodded. "It's perfect!"

"I can't do anything today—I have the country club meeting with my parents tonight."

"It'll take thirty minutes," Dev said.

"You should've warned me."

"Why?"

"Dev, you can't just spring these things on me out of the blue," I snapped. "I'm not a trained monkey."

"C'mon. It's easy and fun. We're going to co-brand you with a really cute boy."

"Oh," I said. Cute boy is really the only motivation a girl in high school needs.

"Look, it's really simple," Dev replied. "The guy will pick you up after school in his car. He's a friend of my sister's from Princeton."

"A college man—I like that," Callie cooed.

"That's exactly the reaction I'm hoping to get from the whole school," Dev answered, her eyes now beginning to sparkle. "And since he's from out of town, no one can ask him if it's for real or not. Perfect, right?"

Credit to Dev—she'd really thought it through. But I didn't like that she'd planned the whole thing without talking to me about it.

"Just trust me on this," Dev said. "When the bell rings after eighth period, make sure you're out front and across from the pick-up lane. Stand under the flag."

"Stand under the American flag?"

"Yeah. Subconsciously people will read it as . . . patriotic."

Callie raised a skeptical eyebrow.

"Okay, maybe not," Dev said, "but it's still the best place to be seen."

She took out a hand-drawn map from her book bag and spread it out on the ground.

"See here?" She pointed. "This is the optimal position. Between the buses lining up over here and the lacrosse team coming out for practice here. And don't forget Will and his boys head out to the parking lot from these doors. So does Gretchen. Standing beneath the flagpole will ensure that just about everyone who needs to notice you being picked up by the incredible college hottie, will."

"I see," I said. It would be nice to give Will a little shove, and even nicer to give Gretchen a little run for her money. Still—this was going to be *way* public.

Sensing that I was feeling skittish, Dev put her hand on mine.

"I promise I'll keep you more in the loop next time," she whispered. "Besides, you can't back out on me."

"Why?"

"I paid the guy three hundred bucks."

When the bell rang at 2:55 p.m., I dashed from my locker

and headed out the west wing, which would deposit me right beside the flagpole and bus line. I had my head down and was making good progress, when a hand grabbed my shoulder.

"Kate," a deep voice said.

I turned around to find Mr. Walsh standing in front of me.

"Oh. Hi, Mr. Walsh."

"I didn't get a chance to talk to you after class the other day," he explained. "I wanted to see how your final paper was coming along."

My final paper. *Right.* Ever since Dev and I had embarked on our little adventure, basic things like homework had totally gone out the window. Granted, we were all skating through senior spring, but there were a few things that did need to get done, like said Econ paper.

"I'm . . . um . . . getting there," I mumbled.

What was I writing it on again?

"I'm glad to hear that. Remember you're giving your oral-presentation portion next week."

"I'm on it—no worries."

"There was actually an interesting article in the *Wall Street Jo*—"

I glanced at my watch—the minutes were ticking away.

"I'm sorry, Mr. Walsh, I gotta bolt." And I took off.

Two weeks ago, I never would've dreamed of cutting

off a teacher mid-sentence, particularly the likes of Mr. Walsh. After all, he had written one of my college recommendations—but these were desperate times.

It was now 3:01 p.m.

When I got to the doors I banged them open and rushed across the street to the flagpole. There was no one there yet, and as I waited, catching my breath, I watched a sea of kids start filing out the east and west wing doors. I glanced up the road, but so far there was only a long line of school buses and a few parents in minivans picking up students. Where was this guy?

It was right then that—just as Dev had predicted—Gretchen Tanner exited via the side door, trailed by Elisa Estrada. Instead of lingering by the curb, where Carrie usually picked them up in her BMW convertible, Gretchen stood by the doors and then glanced over my way, whispering something to Elisa. A second later, she handed Elisa her bag and cruised across the road toward me.

Uh-oh.

"Kate," Gretchen called as she approached, her diamond-encrusted Proud Crowd "P" swinging from its silver chain.

"Hey." I smiled in an attempt to channel someone much calmer and cooler than I.

"I wanted to tell you how much I love your hair."

I studied her for a beat. *Was she for real or was she just messing with me?* My spider senses didn't detect any sarcasm.

"Um . . . thanks."

"Where did you go? Salon Noir?"

"Images."

Gretchen reached out and touched my shoulder. "Carlo is the best!" she cooed. "Don't you love him?"

Okay, this was really weird. Since when had Gretchen decided to get all girlie-girl with me? I glanced around to make sure that I wasn't being filmed or something, but there weren't any cameras; at least any that were visible.

"Yeah, he's awesome."

A squeal of tires pierced the silence, and before I knew what was happening, a black Porsche peeled down the road and screeched to a halt in front of us. A moment later, a cute boy of about nineteen or twenty, sporting a Princeton T-shirt, popped out of the driver's seat and walked over to us. He stared for a few moments, and it took me more than a second to realize he didn't know which one of us was Kat.

"Hey, you're a little late," I said. I thought I detected disappointment in his face when he realized he was picking up the non-bombshell of the two, but he quickly recovered.

"I got held up after class."

Gretchen gave him the once-over, and I could tell she was totally impressed. She looked at me for a second, and then a light went off in her eyes. Maybe she smelled a fake or maybe she had something else in mind, but whatever it was, she wasn't going to accept this at face value.

"Hi, I'm Gretchen," she said, and flipped her hair like we were still in eighth grade. "What dorm are you in at Princeton? Rockefeller? Forbes?"

My pretend boyfriend turned toward Gretchen and all but forgot I was there.

"Wilson, actually," he said, as he held out his hand and she took it. He might as well have been drooling. "I'm Rick Sasson. Are you an alum's daughter or have you come up for a 'fun' college weekend before?"

This was turning out to be gross and humiliating all at the same time. If Dev had actually paid this guy three hundred dollars to be my pretend boyfriend, I was about to demand a full refund. He actually took a step toward her, and you could see the smile spread across her face. Gretchen Tanner was about to steal my boyfriend, albeit my pretend one, in front of the whole school.

I cleared my throat as loud as I could. "Rick, we need to get to that thing?"

"What thing?" he said, not even bothering to look away from Gretchen.

Was this idiot really attending Princeton? I mean, was he on a sports scholarship?

"That three-hundred-dollar thing. Remember that?"

His head snapped toward me, and he had a little fire in his eyes. "Oh yeah, that *desperate* thing we're taking care of together."

"Yeah, that one," I said.

He turned toward Gretchen and gave her a pregnant stare, like he was telekinetically sending his phone number to her. Little did he know Gretchen's brain couldn't hold more than six digits at a time. Then he turned away and handed me the keys.

"You drive," he said.

I got in the front seat—musing that Dev must've put him up to the "you drive" line—and put the key in the ignition and turned it over. The engine roared, and as I looked down to my right, I was immediately thankful that my dad had taught me how to drive a stick shift. I rolled down the passenger window, revealing Gretchen's long legs.

"Gretchen," I shouted. She bent over, bringing her head on level with mine.

"Yeah?"

"See ya around," I said. I slammed the gear shift into first and hit the gas. The tires spun, rocketing us forward, and as I pulled away I looked into my rearview mirror and saw Gretchen standing there dumbfounded in a haze of dust and smoke.

CHAPTER

13

THREE HOURS LATER, Mom, Dad, and I—the very portraits of perfectly coifed suburban happiness—were standing in the parking lot of the Millbank Country Club. No joke, if Norman Rockwell were alive today, he would've painted us for the *Saturday Evening Post* or whatever it was called. We looked *that* annoying. My dad was in a blue Brooks Brothers blazer, pink button-down, and perfectly pressed khakis, while my mom was in pearls and an aqua skirt and blouse. Me? All I can say is that when I caught a glimpse of myself in the window of the Mercedes next to us, I realized that I could've passed for Country Club Barbie.

My sister would've been oh so proud.

"Tuck in the back of your shirt," my mother whispered to Dad.

He sighed and did as he was told. As I said before, Dad (like me) was against this whole thing. Sure, he was a golfer, but he said he enjoyed the public courses and felt no need to join a club. In fact, he was opposed to country clubs in general. The way he put it—just five minutes ago in the car on our way up—they were filled with "limousine liberals" and "created an elitist environment." Had he not been sitting in the front seat, I would've given him a high five, but instead I nodded to myself and stared out the window.

The Millbank Country Club was situated on the top of Ryland Mountain and had views of both the valley below and New York City in the distance. The main clubhouse was surrounded by towering trees, and a huge lawn rolled all the way down the hill to the stone and wrought-iron gates.

"Can I help you?" the boy behind the reception desk said as we entered the vaulted foyer. A precocious master of the snotty how-must-I-help-you voice, he couldn't have been a day over sixteen, but he acted as if he had the keys to the universe. I will admit, however, that he was cute in that ultra-preppy way, so he kind of got away with it.

"We're here to see Mr. Biddle," Mom said with a smile.

Cute Snobby Guy opened a black leather-bound book and ran his finger down the page. "Yes, the Winthrops," he noted. "Would you wait in the tea room?"

He didn't look up at us, mind you—just pointed to a

room off to the side—and like cows being herded to slaughter, we wandered over.

The "tea room"—as it was so incongruously named—was about the size of a basketball court. At the far end of the room, a few families were having drinks, and a waiter cruised by with a silver tray full of food. Mahogany paneling covered the walls and ornate chandeliers dangled from the ceiling, giving the room a warm, yellowish glow. Hanging throughout the room were series of framed reprints by Manet and various other Impressionists. Over the stone fireplace was a five-foot-tall portrait of Taylor Millbank, the grandson of the town's founder and the first president of the club in 1896, and next to it hung a large photograph of Dan Tanner—the current president of the club.

Barely able to contain her excitement, my mother sat down primly in one of the overstuffed leathers and positioned herself on the edge of the seat with her hands on her knees. I'm telling you, it was like she'd teleported in a version of herself from the 1950s. For my own part, I dropped into the sofa with my father and fiddled with the burgundy matchbooks emblazoned with the MCC logo.

I couldn't wait to get out of there.

Fifteen minutes later I was still fiddling with the matchbooks because we were still waiting for Mr. Biddle. Cute Snobby Guy from the reception desk poked his head in and announced that Mr. Biddle was delayed and it would be yet another fifteen minutes, but my mother smiled as if nothing were wrong and told the boy that would be "totally fine."

A few minutes later, the fireworks began.

"This is exactly the sort of nonsense I hate," my father hissed.

"What are you talking about?" my mother asked without breaking her smile, like she was worried there were surveillance cameras watching us or something.

"The elitism. The 'we're better than you' attitude," he started. "You know, all these people who are members here moved to Millbank presumably for its diversity of people, cultures, and activities. And what do they do? They cloister themselves up here on the mountain."

"Don't be ridiculous," she answered.

She was still smiling.

"I don't have all night to wait around for these people. Frankly, I'd like to watch the Yankees game at seven."

"Yeah, and I have to be at work soon," I chimed in.

Mom fidgeted in her seat, but refused to respond to either of us.

Taking her cue, I pulled out my cell phone and called information for the number of the Millbank Taxi and Limousine service.

"If you make that call, Kate," Mom whispered, "you'll regret it." She had a sharp little look in her eye that said she meant business.

I hung up and hit the speed dial for the BookStop. Howie answered after fifteen rings.

"Fidel," I said. "It's Che. I'm in the den of the enemy and running late."

"Where are you, Kate?" he asked.

"The Millbank Country Club."

There was a long pause on the phone and then a loaded sigh. A beat later there was a click. He actually hung up in my face. Well . . . I'd deal with that later.

"What did he say?" Mom said.

"He felt sick at the mere mention of the Millbank Club and hung up," I said.

"Kate! Someone might hear you!"

"I don't care, Mom! I hate this club."

"Well, then," Mr. Biddle said, walking into the room.

I couldn't tell if he'd heard me, but Mom gave me a death-ray stare, and I slumped back into the sofa.

"Sorry to keep you waiting. My sincerest apologies."

My mother, who had apparently been doing research among her female friends, told me in advance that not only was Mr. Biddle the club manager, he was also quite the hit with the ladies of the club. Now I understood what she meant. Dark hair with a sprinkle of white, slate gray eyes that were bright against his tanned skin, and a muscular body—I could see why bored housewives would go for him.

He opened a file that was labeled WINTHROPS and began the interview by prattling on about the club, its history, the type of members who joined, blah, blah, blah. He asked us what members we knew (although I'm sure that had been on the ten-page application my father had filled out), if either Mom or Dad were four-o's (tennis lingo, I think), and inquired if we belonged to any other clubs and organizations. Mom and Dad volleyed back answers, and I have to say it seemed to start off smoothly.

"Excellent," Mr. Biddle said. "Now, tell me. Why do you think you would make good members for the club?"

I could feel my father tense up next to me, but my mother jumped in, talking about her community service, my father's job in New York, and—I *never* would've guessed it—my sister, who was sorority president.

"So you have two daughters. Of course," Mr. Biddle remarked. "You must be Kate?"

I perked up and nodded.

"What year are you in?"

"I'm a senior, sir."

"Ah, our little Gretchen is a senior, too," he said.

Little Gretchen? To hear him say it, you would've thought she was some poor defenseless soul—like one of those "sponsor a child" kids from Africa.

He scrawled something on his paper, which no doubt was "ask Gretchen about Kate," and Mom started to fidget.

She looked down at me, her eyes widening ever so slightly in an urgent prompting for me to say something.

"Gretchen . . . *Tanner*?" I queried like someone in Special Ed. Biddle nodded. "Yes, I know her."

"Gretchen's the daughter of our current president."

No kidding. Like I missed the billboard over the fireplace.

"She's delightful," I said out of desperation. "We're in Econ together. She's *very* bright."

Mr. Biddle nodded, and I couldn't tell if he believed my lie. "Now, Mr. Winthrop, can you tell me a little more about your line of work?"

It was right then that I saw Will. He walked in through one of the French doors and was a little sweaty and wearing tennis whites, like he'd just finished a game. In that moment, I couldn't decide if I wanted him to see me or not, but as he walked across the room, he spotted me and smiled. He was cruising right over to us.

Omigod.

"Mr. Biddle," Will said as he arrived. "You wanted me?"

"Will!" Mr. Biddle beamed. "Yes, while I'm talking with the Winthrops, would you mind showing their daughter around the club?"

Did Will work here?

"Of course," Will said. "I actually know Kate from school. She's friends with Gretchen and me."

"Really? How terrific," Mr. Biddle replied with a grin.

He jotted something else down on his paper—this time, no doubt, something good.

While I felt myself growing faint from excitement, across from me, my mother lit up like a neon sign. I'm sure she thought having me as far away from Mr. Biddle was a good thing.

I rose to my feet, and Will winked before gesturing toward the hall. "Right this way, Miss Winthrop."

Maybe this country club thing wasn't so bad after all.

"Your parents are thinking of joining the club?" Will asked as he walked me down the stairs to the game room. It had a low ceiling and was filled with pool, Ping-Pong, and foos-ball tables.

"Yeah," I said. "It seems kind of cool." The words just slipped out, like another person inside of me was speaking.

Hadn't I just said to Howie how much I despised this club?

"My mom's really into it," I added, not sure how the MCC fit in with my new "Kat" persona. "And . . . well . . . you know."

As evidence has shown, when it came to talking to Will, I basically reverted to a third-grade idiot. Granted, I was pretty smooth that night at Café Electric, but there I felt like I'd been playing a role—everything had been scripted for me by Callie—and, of course . . . it was dark. Here in the bright lights of the country club, I felt exposed, and worse, that cotton-mouth feeling returned. Still, I forced myself to keep talking.

"So you work here?"

He shrugged his shoulders. "Part time during the school year. Full time in the summers. . . I mean, it's better than paying the $10,000 initiation fee."

"Wow."

I must have looked surprised, because he quickly added, "It's more for adults and families, like $25,000."

No wonder my dad was against the whole idea.

I looked up at Will, who was now racking the loose balls on the pool table. It kind of hit me again, like a sting seconds after a slap, but he worked here. It must have been awkward for him among the Proud Crowd, who were all members. Did he serve them drinks? Did he get them towels at the pool? Every day seemed to bring me a new revelation about the *famous* Will B.

I followed Will back upstairs and we walked through a marble foyer past the patio, which was lit up blue from the lights in the pool. It was still a little cold for swimming, but a thin steam rose off the water, where a few diehards were doing laps. We turned left down a long hallway that finally opened onto a gigantic ballroom. A huge crystal chandelier hung from the middle of the ceiling, and through the glass windows that lined the back wall, you could see Manhattan beginning to twinkle in the distance. Will flicked on a switch, and the chandelier glowed to life.

"And this"—Will motioned to the room—"is where the Black & White Ball is held."

The Black & White Ball. He said it like he was talking to a foreigner. Everybody knew it was held here. It was *the* biggest social event in Millbank; bigger than homecoming, bigger than your birthday, bigger than Christmas. The true origins of the Black & White Ball stretched back to before Truman Capote (the guy who wrote *Breakfast at Tiffany's*) threw his big party in New York in the 1960s. MCC legend had it, in fact, that Capote stole the idea from *them*. Basically it was a masquerade where everyone wore either—yes, you guessed it—black or white, and let me tell you, people in Millbank went all out. The night of the ball, you'd always see people walking to their cars dressed to the nines, while others were chauffeured to the top of the hill. For seniors at Millbank, on the first Saturday of June, it was the only place to be. Assuming, of course, you were invited. It was for members only and their guests.

"Have you been to it?" I asked.

"What?"

"The ball."

"Totally," Will answered as he turned off the light. "It's cool. But it's also not the big thing that everyone makes it out to be."

"How do you mean?"

He shook his head and didn't meet my eye. "It just isn't exactly my scene."

I can't tell you why exactly, but there was something in his answer that made him seem . . . well . . . human for the first time. Up until that point Will had always been, you know, *Will B.*, dream guy. And now that I was seeing him tread upon the earth—metaphorically speaking, of course— what had just been an infatuation shifted into something more. I could feel my heart in my throat.

"I'm surprised you've never been," he added.

"My sister went. All four years in high school," I revealed stupidly. I hated being compared to her in any way, and here I'd just lined it up. I looked away and stared down at the carpet.

"Melissa, right?" Will asked, and I nodded. "Yeah, I remember her. She was really cute."

I said nothing. Like I hadn't heard that from every guy to whom I had ever spoken.

"But you've got something she doesn't."

Stop. The. Press. Did Will just tell me what I think he told me?

I'm sure I went bright red, but I kept looking down at the floor.

"You don't have to say that."

He reached out and lifted my chin. "But it's true."

Someone catch me when I fall!

"But I'm sure your boyfriend has told you that before."

"Boyfriend?"

"You know," he said, "that guy who picked you up this afternoon."

Oh, yeah, that boyfriend!

"He's not my boyfriend," I confessed. "I mean, we've gone out a couple times, but it's not, like, serious or anything."

Will cocked his head to the side. "This is probably going to sound weird, but I'm glad to hear that."

I smiled, despite myself, and Will kept staring at me.

"Will." I heard a man's voice call. I looked down the hall, and Mr. Biddle was approaching with my parents. Truthfully, it was probably a good thing, because I had no idea what I would've done next.

"How was your tour, Kate?" my mother asked as she entered the room.

"It was great." I glanced over at Will. "Will's a wonderful guide."

Mr. Biddle nodded with appreciation, and Will ran his hand through his hair. "Think about what I said," he said with a little grin.

And I did—the whole rest of the night. I was so over the moon about my conversation with Will that I totally forgot to go to my shift at the BookStop. Instead, I sat at my desk in my room, staring out the window across the tops of the maple trees, and never fell asleep.

······························

KCW LLC.

MARKET RANKING: 43
TODAY'S CHANGE: ↑7

SHARE PRICE: $6.95
    CHANGE: ↑.20 (+2.9%)
L/B RATIO: 5.3
3-MONTH RANGE: $1.23 – $7.01
STATUS: COMMON STOCK

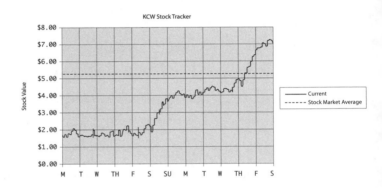

KCW Stock Tracker

ANALYST RECOMMENDATION: This stock is taking off faster than a Porsche. Well-heeled investors are apparently already getting in on this—you should, too.

BUY

······························

CHAPTER

14

SATURDAY NIGHT, I was due to meet Jack for our Dickey Dogs outing. I'd actually been looking forward to my chowdown with Jack, but with the turn of events at the country club with Will, I felt a little less certain. Part of me considered canceling, but I couldn't bring myself to do it, so we agreed to meet at the BookStop at seven p.m. I needed to pick up my paycheck anyway.

"So lovely of you to grace us with your presence today," Howie drawled as I walked in.

Even though I'd called Mrs. Sawyer earlier in the day to apologize for missing work, I knew that Howie's anger wouldn't dissipate so simply.

"I know, I'm sorry," I said, and made a face like I was the biggest idiot ever.

"What-*ever*," he answered. "Clearly a girl who's going to be joining the Millbank Country Club doesn't need a job."

"Mea culpa. It won't happen again."

"That's what you say now, but there have been more than a handful of radicals who sold out when a better opportunity came along. I'm starting to worry that you'll soon be joining their ranks."

"C'mon, Howie. Do I look like a sellout?"

As soon as I said it, I realized that in the vintage von Furstenberg wrap dress and leather boots that Callie had picked out for me, I didn't exactly look like one of Chairman Mao's foot soldiers. He was silent.

"Fine. Fine. Point taken," I acknowledged. "But it was my mother's idea, remember? She's the one who insisted that I go there. What could I do?"

He picked up his pen and pointed down at me. "The Nuremberg defense only goes so far."

I didn't know what the Nuremberg defense was exactly—was it some chess move?—and I stood there for a few moments blinking. After a beat, Howie waved me away.

"Never mind, I'll just start calling you Eva Braun from now on," he sulked. "Your check is in the back."

I didn't want to push the argument too far, but it wasn't lost on me that Howie wears Air Jordans when he plays hoops at the Y. They are the male equivalent of

Blahniks, after all (I know all the utilitarian arguments—
sorry, they don't fly!), so I wasn't sure that he was entirely in
the right. As I wandered to the back, I found I was actually
a little surprised by how hard Howie had come down
on me.

"You ready?" I called to Jack, who had his back to me
and was digging through a box of books.

"Hey," he said as he stood up, and a totally cute alarm
went off in my head. He was wearing well-worn khakis, a
dress shirt, and his hair was perfectly messy—I was certain
it must've taken him an hour to get it so ratty.

"So," I said, a little nervous now.

"Let's roll."

Dickey Dogs was the type of place that in another era
would've probably been called "a joint." On the border of
Belleville and Newark, it had originally been an old North
Ward Italian mainstay until some kids discovered it,
embraced its kitchiness, and turned it into a hangout. It certainly wasn't the coolest place to be, but for a certain set it
had become a must-visit destination on any night out.

What was the appeal, you might ask? For some, it was
the photographs of old-school Italian dudes on the wall, but
for most it was the Dickey Dog—which actually was a bit
of a misnomer. A Dickey (as it was called) was not one, but
two hot dogs, deep-fried in oil, smothered in fried peppers

and onions, and then topped with fried potatoes and stuffed into a hollowed-out hoagie roll (which was the sole part of the sandwich that *wasn't* fried). Nasty as it may sound, it was, in fact, totally tasty, but you could never dream of eating more than one.

The evening with Jack thus far had been . . . well . . . uneventful. Sweet he was, and he certainly was a gentleman of the highest order—opening every door, even pulling out my chair at the table—but he also wasn't exactly what you'd call thrilling. He always seemed a little tense, like there was something percolating deep down that he just couldn't quite get out.

"So that's where you were? The Millbank Country Club?"

As Jack seemed trustworthy enough, I'd confided in him about the reason for my no-show at work.

"It's okay," he noted as he took a sip from his soda. "But it's kind of a scene."

"You're a member?" I asked, surprised.

"Yeah, sort of. My dad joined for business reasons; we never really go, though. It's not my thing."

"Oh, that's what Will said."

"He isn't a member," Jack replied, his eyebrow nudging up.

"No, I know—I mean that it wasn't his thing. Actually, he said the Black & White wasn't his thing."

Jack looked up at me and squinted. "Huh."

Something told me that I was wading into deep waters, so I steered things back toward the shore. "Well, I always heard it was really great."

"You could totally come with me, if you wanted," Jack suddenly offered in his trademark earnest way. "I've never taken anyone."

I couldn't believe it. Three weeks before, I would've jumped at the offer—like bounced off the ceiling to get an invite—but something within me checked my excitement. Much as I didn't want to admit it, I guess I was hoping Will might figure out a way to take me, as far-fetched as that might be.

"Sure, uh, maybe," I mused as I fiddled with my straw.

Jack seemed unfazed by my hedge. "No worries. Think about it."

No commitment, no foul; that was my philosophy. And since I couldn't think of a clever response, I changed the subject. "So what's the background on Jack Clayton? You're a bit of a cipher."

Jack shrugged his shoulders. "What do you want to know?"

"Let's start with the guitar."

"My parents had me take piano lessons growing up. I taught myself to play guitar."

"Impressive."

"Not really," he said, but something in his eyes made me think he was being very modest. "It's really not that hard."

"For me it would be. I'm tone deaf," I joked. "I think I got it from my mother. She always jokes that people used to make fun of her when she tried to sing me lullabies."

"Actually, there's no such thing as being tone deaf," Jack noted. "It's just a myth."

"I'm happy to prove that it's a reality."

He laughed. "And then Will and I started jamming together in seventh grade, and you know the rest."

Trying to act as casual as possible, I adjusted my bracelet.

"So that must be cool, playing in the band."

"Yeah, I really like what we do. Music has always been a refuge. . . ." Jack trailed off and gazed down at his food.

"Will's a good songwriter."

Jack's eyes flashed my way. "He doesn't write."

"Oh," I said. When I was watching them play last week, Will made it seem like he owned the songs, like they had to be his. "Sorry, I just assumed."

"Whatever," he said. "I'm playing by myself on Friday. I don't have the pipes Will does, but I'm okay."

"Oh, I'll come," I said spontaneously.

"Really?"

I thought for a beat. There was something about Jack that

intrigued me. What was that saying? *Still waters run deep?*

"Absolutely."

"Cool." His mouth creaked into a smile for all of a second.

I glanced away and surveyed the room while he finished eating. The place was packed mostly with kids our age, and there were more people than I could count from Millbank. Peppered among the crowd were some old Italians—people who had clearly come here long before it had become a trendy spot for hipsters—and they eyed the younger crowd with a palpable disgust. I'm sure they were less than pleased that their local spot had become overrun. Even the owner practically snarled at you when you ordered, but I guess he wasn't complaining when he went to the bank.

"So can I ask *you* a question?" he said.

I raised my eyebrows as if to say, Well, go ahead.

"What's with 'Kat'?"

The question threw me, and for a moment I struggled for a response. His directness was unsettling.

"I guess I just felt like a change," I answered and popped a French fry into my mouth.

"Tired of being you, then?"

"That sounds right."

"Were you unhappy?"

"What gives, Sigmund?" I laughed.

"Sorry."

I took a deep breath and stared down at the manicure I'd gotten the week before. The polish was chipping away, like my self-confidence. *Why was I getting wound up?* His questions were simple enough—not even remotely offensive—but for some reason they were striking a raw nerve. Something about Jack was challenging, like he was pushing me. I kind of liked it, but at the same time, I wanted to push him away.

"Sorry," I said. "We all have ten selves for ten different situations."

"I understand," Jack replied. "I'm totally different onstage. But for the record, I like *this* you best."

I blushed, or at least I felt the heat in my cheeks. I knew he meant he liked me and not Kat, or the previous mute Katie, and for some reason that made my heart swell more. He was so sincere, so guileless.

"All this won't make you happy—only you can make you happy," he said.

"Jack," I began, unable to meet his gaze. "You're so sweet."

As soon as I said it, I knew it came out the wrong way; like I was being patronizing.

He shook his head. "Weird how a nice word can mean such a bad thing."

"No," I whispered. "It . . . I like the things you say."

He stared at me for a moment, and for the first time I

didn't break away. A beat later—calmly and gently—he leaned over the table and kissed me on the lips. We parted, faces still close, and my heart fluttered, and . . . I kissed him again.

And then something happened that was both unexpected, and now, looking back, so deeply sad. I was kissing Jack Clayton in Dickey Dogs, my heart was pounding, my face flushing, and all I could think of was one thing:

My Market rating is going to go through the roof.

CHAPTER

15

ON MONDAY, no mention of the kiss fest at Dickey Dogs appeared on the Market, but there was another bounce in my numbers. It seemed that nothing could stunt my ascension. Not even Jodi Letz trying to spread rumors about me becoming bulimic (she was inadvertently named as a "source" for one of the INSIDER INFORMATION tips). Nope, according to Callie—who was our "portfolio manager"—our little enterprise was taking off, and one by one, we were surpassing the other portfolios on the Market. Sure, we still had a ways to go, but the three of us had already figured out how we were going to spend the $25,000. There was only one other portfolio (TKWP Enterprises) that was doing as well as us, but we weren't worried because we had Dev's plan to fall back on.

With the bit officially between her teeth—and dollar signs in her eyes—Dev was like a girl possessed. It was a little disturbing, actually. Aside from her usual plotting and constantly calling me with Market updates—"they loved the pigtail look!"—Dev arrived at my house one afternoon and plopped down a stack of highlighted business books that I was supposed to review (yeah, right!) as part of my business education. *Good to Great*, *The Art of the Deal*, *The Art of War*, *Winning*, bios of Donald Trump, Warren Buffet, and Steve Jobs—it was a big stack. She said that if I wanted to make it to the top, I needed to learn how the masters of the universe had done it.

Despite my intense focus on climbing the Market, I couldn't shake the image of Jack and me kissing. There wasn't any shift in our relationship—we weren't suddenly dating or anything like that—but what he'd said really stuck with me. Was he right? Was the "normal" me better? Not according to the Market. Still, a little voice inside my head tried to sound a warning cry about the road Dev and I had chosen, but I told myself over and over that the proof was in the numbers.

The topic in Econ class that Thursday was ethics in the business world. The list of disgraced businessmen—as you might imagine—is a long one, and Mr. Walsh trotted out a cavalcade of names and companies to demonstrate how bad bad can be. Charles Ponzi (he's the guy who invented the

Pyramid Scheme), Ken Lay (he drove that company Enron into the ground by lying about profits), oil companies that ran private militias in Africa to advance their interests, General Electric dumping waste into the Hudson River in the 1970s, businesses that outsourced manufacturing to Southeast Asia so they could hire cheap child labor—it went on and on. The greed for a dollar seemingly knew no boundaries, and the lengths to which people would go for a few more, extreme. By the middle of class, we'd gotten to the stock market and, specifically, insider trading.

"While it's the Securities and Exchange Commission's job to monitor suspicious trading, the eighties were a period rife with illegal stock market activity," Mr. Walsh explained.

"Isn't that what Martha Stewart did?" Elisa Estrada asked.

"Accused of," Mr. Walsh corrected. "She was only ever convicted of lying to authorities. But, yes, the idea behind insider trading is that someone has privileged information about a company and buys or sells stock based on that."

Gretchen snorted and rolled her eyes. "Isn't that just called being connected?"

"It's called breaking the law," Mr. Walsh answered without missing a beat. "And many people have gone to jail for it. Ivan Boesky, Michael Milken, David—"

"Michael Milken?" I exclaimed.

That was the screen name of the person who first IMed me about the Market!

"You've heard of him before, Kate?"

"I guess I read about him," I covered, when I realized that half the class was staring at me. "What did he do exactly?"

Mr. Walsh leaned back on his desk and folded his arms. "It's complicated, but basically he made his fortune in the junk bond market. He'd invest in poorly rated securities, drive their value up, and then sell them at a huge profit. He made billions."

A junk bond. Wasn't that what I was first rated on the Market?

"Is he still in business?"

"No, he does philanthropy or something now," Mr. Walsh replied with a chuckle. "So moving on, if we look at—"

Obviously the person who IMed me wasn't the real Michael Milken—like he'd care about Millbank High School—so it must've been someone who identified with him somehow. And what did it mean in terms of me and the Market?

It was right then that there was a quick knock at the door and a moment later, much to my surprise, Dev walked in. Her face looked sad, her eyes a little puffy, and she crossed to Mr. Walsh and handed him a note. They conferred for a moment, and he opened the piece of paper.

His expression fell, and he nodded grimly.

"Ms. Winthrop," he said, "please go with Ms. Rayner."

What happened?

Concern coursed through me, and I quickly packed up my stuff and walked to the front of the room. Dev put her arm around my back and whispered loudly into my ear.

"I'm so sorry. Your grandfather died."

There was a palpable inhale from the students in the front row, who'd heard it all, and I just stared at her. I'm certain that my face must've looked like a truck had just run me over, and after a beat, I glanced over at Mr. Walsh, who reached over and patted my back a few times.

"I'm so sorry," he said.

I didn't know what to do, and I felt my chest convulse a few times—a vague feeling of nausea overtook me. I covered my mouth. I could feel the eyes of the class on me, so I ran out and across the hallway and into the bathroom. Dev rushed after me. When the door closed and we were alone, I turned toward her.

"How could you?" I hissed.

"It was perfect!" Dev grinned back.

Let me explain: I never knew my grandfather. Both my parents' parents had passed away long before I was born. Despite the conversation we'd had, Dev had blatantly gone against my wishes and invented a tragedy for "brand loyalty" or whatever. Never, ever, ever would I have gone along with it, but with Mr. Walsh looking at me so sympathetically and the whole class staring straight at me, what could I do? Expose Dev and have her get in trouble for falsely conveying info to get me out of class? No, I wasn't going to rat out my friend, but she had crossed the line.

"I told you I didn't want to do Step Three," I said angrily. "We didn't need it."

Just then the door to the girls' bathroom creaked open, and Dev shoved me into one of the stalls and shut it.

"Hey," I heard a voice. "How is she?"

"She's really upset," Dev replied. "But she'll be fine— I'm going to take her home."

I heard the door open again, and while somebody left, the sound of heels clicking indicated a few others coming in.

"Omigod, is she okay?" I heard Gretchen Tanner ask, followed by a barrage of queries from her posse of chicks, who'd obviously followed like sheep to inquire about my emotional well-being.

Standing there in the stall, staring at the scrawl on the back of the door, I felt sick about the whole thing, but I stayed silent. If I said anything now, I'd only look like a complete and total liar. In those next ten minutes, while word was seemingly passed throughout the school and more and more people came to check on me, all my concerns and anxiety about what we had been doing came back to roost deep in my chest. If I'd been able to justify what we'd been doing up until now, I couldn't anymore.

It was going too far. It had to stop.

Shortly, the bell for next class rang, and finally the bathroom emptied. I walked out of the stall and snatched my bag from the tile floor where it lay.

"Let's get out of here," Dev whispered.

"Don't talk to me!"

I stormed out of the bathroom, and we headed to the car. I kept my head down, and I'm sure people thought I was crying, but I was really just trying to avoid eye contact. The thought of people feeling sympathy for me because Dev had faked a tragedy made me feel sick to my stomach.

When we got outside to the parking lot, Callie was waiting for us at Dev's car. Seeing me so clearly pissed, she shook her head.

"I knew she'd be upset!" she shouted as I approached. "I knew you two would regret this!"

"I'm out," I said as I wheeled around on Dev. "I'm out of this crazy game. No more clothes, no more new Kate, no more Market."

"What are you talking about?"

"When I said I didn't want to fake a tragedy, I meant it. I don't want to be a fraud! How could you?!"

Her faced dropped. She had no real response. She just stared at me with big teary eyes that slowly overflowed.

"I didn't think," she said. "I didn't. I'm sorry."

"Pathetic," I said.

Irony of all ironies, I thought as I slipped into my car and gunned the engine to life. Dev stages a fake tragedy to help me, but the only real victim was our friendship.

KCW LLC.

MARKET RANKING: 32
TODAY'S CHANGE: ↑7

SHARE PRICE: $11.56
CHANGE: ↑4.31 (+62.7%)
L/B RATIO: 5.3
3-MONTH RANGE: $1.23 – $11.62
STATUS: PREFERRED STOCK

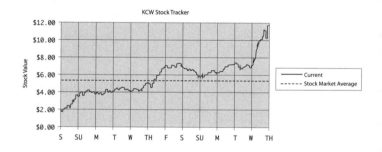

ANALYST RECOMMENDATION: Tragedy may have struck, but investors are more exuberant than ever. Blue Chip status is within reach for this stunning mover.

STRONG BUY

CHAPTER

16

No matter how I may have felt about what Dev and Callie had done, one thing was for sure: it worked.

When I checked my e-mail that night, I had about fifty messages from people saying how sorry they were to hear about the death in my family, wanting to know if I was okay, and if there was anything they could do. It was unbelievable! Half the people I barely even knew. Was I less unpopular than I thought, or had Dev dialed into what made people tick? I'm still not sure, but either way, Callie later told me that word spread like wildfire through the school. Students and teachers had come up to her and Dev the whole rest of the day, asking about what had happened and wanting to get the whole story. Needless to say, they didn't exactly give anyone a straight answer, but that only baited people more. The less information she gave them, the more they wanted to know about it.

But as I scanned through the e-mails and listened to the *dings* of incoming sympathy, I couldn't help it: I felt dirty. For starters—and I'm not a superstitious person—it seemed like really bad karma to go around lying about death. But more importantly, it just felt wrong. It was manipulation of the worst kind, and although I remembered all of Dev's justifications, I didn't want any part of it.

There was a quick knock at my door, and as I spun around in my desk chair, my dad poked his head in the room.

"You have a sec?" he asked.

I nodded before shooting a glance around my room, and I noticed that it was only 6:30 p.m., about an hour earlier than my father usually got home. Not a good sign, but truthfully, I already had an idea what this was going to be about.

"What's up?" I asked.

He put his hands in his pockets and glanced up at the ceiling for a moment—his telltale sign for "We're going to have a serious conversation."

"I got the strangest call from Principal Johnson this afternoon," he began. "Do you have any idea what it might have been about?"

It was that classic moment when you know you're about

to get busted by your parents, and you're faced with the unenviable choice of either copping to it, or issuing the bald-faced lie of a flat-out denial. I chose the former.

"I'm sorry. It wasn't even my idea—"

Before I could get started, he put up his hand. "I'm sure it's a very long and convoluted story, and frankly, I don't have time to hear it. I have to take your mother to buy a new vacuum cleaner."

"What?"

"Don't ask," he silenced me. "Anyway . . . I didn't say anything to Johnson, because I don't want to put your academic status in jeopardy."

"Thank you!"

"But I do suspect that this stunt you and your friends pulled has something to do with this new . . . 'persona' you've adopted."

I stared down at my carpeting on the floor. Obviously he was right on the money.

"I want it to stop. *Now.* Are we clear?"

I nodded. "I'd already decided that anyway."

"Good."

Before my father could say anything more, the doorbell rang, and we looked at each other quizzically.

"You want to go see who that is?" he asked.

I shrugged my shoulders, and with Remington trailing at my heels, I padded my way down the steps to the front hall and opened the door. Oddly, there was no one there. Down the street, I could hear the whine of an engine zooming away, and it wasn't until I glanced down at my feet that I discovered there was a modestly wrapped gift leaning against the doorjamb. I picked it up, and as I held it in my hands, I realized almost immediately it was a book.

I closed the door and made my way into the kitchen, where I unwrapped the present. It was a copy of *A Grief Observed* by C. S. Lewis.

C. S. Lewis? The guy who wrote *The Chronicles of Narnia*?

I thumbed to the title page and saw that there was an inscription.

> I was really sorry to hear about your grandfather today. I never know what to say in these situations, but someone gave me this book when my mom died—maybe it'll make you feel better.
> Best,
> Jack

I just sat there for a few moments, staring at what Jack had written. Once again the master of understatement, his gesture was incredibly touching—and it only made me feel worse about everything that had gone down.

Yes, it was official. Kat was off the Market.

CHAPTER

17

I DIDN'T HAVE too much time to rehash my decision, because Friday I was due to give the oral presentation portion of my final project for Econ. My paper was on Horatio Alger—he wrote a series of rags-to-riches novels in the 1900s—and how the idea of what constitutes success has changed in America over the last century. It used to be that all you needed was some middle-class security and a good reputation. Obviously, we all know it isn't that way anymore. Anyway, Thursday night mainly consisted of going over my notes, making charts, and even drawing a graph depicting the relationship between GDP and wealth on a piece of poster board. (What can I say, I'm a fan of visual aids.)

Before I went to bed, I felt the need to reclaim a little

of the old Kate, so I woke up my computer and hopped online. There were a bunch of IMs from Dev, apologizing for the day, but I still wasn't quite up for dealing with her, so I didn't reply, and instead I logged on to my Gmail account. I shot Jack an e-mail thanking him for the book and told him that I'd definitely be there for his solo show tomorrow night. There was also a note from Callie, claiming, and I believed her, that she tried to talk Dev out of the fake tragedy. At least I didn't have to feel betrayed by two friends.

I arrived at school the next day, happily resigned to wherever I was on the Market—not that I had any intention of ever looking at it again. Nope, I'd put it in the ground for good, kind of like what you'd do with an obnoxious ex-boyfriend who called you fat.

To be honest, it was a relief to be done with Dev's master plan. While I had no intention of symbolically burning my new wardrobe beneath the flagpole (a girl can be contrite and still look good), the knowledge that there wasn't another task around the corner was a load off my mind. Yes, there was part of me that still wondered what it would've been like to be a Blue Chip. And yes, I found it hard to let go of the fantasy of every boy in the school swooning when I passed. And yes, it pained me to finally get a taste of the popular life and have that snatched away, but something my father was fond of saying hung in my mind like a banner: "Character requires sacrifice." So if I had to sacrifice Kat in order to hold my head high, that was the way it was going to be.

It was after third period that I was standing at my locker, trying to slip my poster in without crushing it under the load of books and boots and magazines and makeup that filled my measly six-inch by forty-eight-inch box, when I felt a tap on my shoulder. A second later, a droopy-eyed Will leaned against the locker next to mine.

"Hey."

"Hi," I replied, catching a glimpse of myself in the mirror I'd taped to the inside of my locker door. Thank God I hadn't done anything crazy that day like swearing off makeup.

"I'm really sorry," he whispered.

I smiled. "About what?"

"Your grandfather."

Oh.

Right.

I allowed my gaze to drop to the floor and I nodded. "Thanks. It was a real . . . shock."

For the first time in my life I appreciated President Clinton's mastery of the evasive response that neither confirmed nor denied.

"Things like that can be really hard," he continued. "It sucks. There's not much else to say about it."

A gaggle of cute sophomore girls bounced by—pert and carefree—with the requisite "Hi, Will," and he waved back at them.

"Listen," he said as the hall began to clear, "I know this is going to sound a little weird, but do you want to get out of here?"

"And go where?" I asked.

This is strange.

"Get out—blow off the day."

I laughed. "Cut? Why?"

"I don't know . . . sometimes it's 'why not?'" he said as a mischievous grin crept across his face. "It's Kat—not Katie, right?"

By now my mind was beginning to race. The Kat versus Katie button was the one to push. Add that I was struggling with this small question: was Will asking me to hang?

"That's sweet, but . . ." I paused, somehow summoning the courage for the truth. "The grandfather thing was a—"

Will cut me off before I could spill the beans.

"I bet you've been here four years and never cut just for the hell of it."

It wasn't every day that someone like Will asked me to blow off school and hang out. In fact, no one had ever asked me. It also wasn't every day that I was supposed to do an oral presentation in Econ.

"I can't," I answered like the true geek that I was

beneath the blond hair and the cool clothes. "Besides, I'm sure one of your friends will be up for it."

"They will," he said. "But I'm only up for you."

That was a knee-buckler!

Still hesitating, I leaned against my locker and coyly gazed at him. "Until two weeks ago, we'd said maybe three words to each other. What's up with the mad rush?"

His eyes sparkled and he backed away with a playful shrug. Apparently, he wasn't accustomed to girls calling him out, but he recovered faster than I expected.

"Are you taking a pass?" he said. He was throwing down the gauntlet—it was now or never. Forever Katie? Or did this Kat have a few more lives to live?

I shot a look into my locker—at my poster and the presentation I was supposed to give—and knew that if I bailed on Econ the fallout could be big, but not world-ending; after all, I was a senior in my final three weeks of school. The familiar part of me that had guided my high school career to a 3.8 GPA and admission to Brown hammered away at my conscience, reminding me that under no circumstances could I cut out on school. At the same time, another part of me pointed out that this modus operandi also had led me to many dateless Friday nights, a junk-bond status on the Market, and a severe jean jacket dependency.

Going with Will, I thought. Definitely going with Will!

* * *

Unlike most of the Proud Crowd, Will did not own a brand-
new, German-engineered, ultimate driving machine.
Instead, he piloted our way east in a rattling and rusting,
but impossibly cool 1974 Triumph Spitfire convertible.
More rocket sled than automobile, the Spitfire lacked the
basics—a roof of any sort, air conditioning, non-splitting
seats—and the feel of certain death clawed my chest whenever Will took a turn too fast. Yet on the straighter roads
with the wind roaring in my ears and my hair unwillingly
crafting itself into a bird's nest, I couldn't help but feel like
I was being squired by a movie star.

When you're cutting school, staying in your hometown
is obviously out of the question, and come one o'clock, as the
speedometer dropped below forty-five, we zoomed out of the
Lincoln Tunnel and headed to downtown Manhattan. With a
confident familiarity, he zipped down Ninth Avenue and then
over to Soho and parked the car on a cobblestone side street.

We spent the next few hours walking around. First we
walked uptown and grabbed a falafel at Mamoun's in the
West Village, then over to Gear, a cool skateboarding store
on Houston, and we even contemplated seeing the new Wes
Anderson film at the Angelika Film Center. Ultimately, we
bailed when we realized we'd be out at seven-fifteen, but a
little part of me likes to think that we skipped it because we
were having so much fun just talking to each other.

Contrary to my previous experiences with Will, where I always lost the capacity to speak, as the hours wore on I found myself growing more and more comfortable around him. Maybe it was being in a totally different context where I felt on equal footing, and he felt like he could just be himself and not "Will B.," but for the first time I was able to see him more as a boy than as the near demigod he was in the halls of Millbank High School.

I extracted tidbits of information about Will that I'd never known before. They didn't always jibe with the person I'd presumed him to be, but this opening of closed doors only made him all the more captivating. It ranged from the humorous—as a boy he'd been fat—to the weird—he ate peanut butter sandwiches with thinly sliced apples on toast almost every night—to the enigmatic—he'd been writing poetry since he was in sixth grade.

"Why don't you write songs, then?" I asked, thinking of what Jack had said.

"I do—Jack and I do," he countered. He looked at me strangely, like perhaps this question had come up before.

"Oh, right," I said.

Why would Jack lie about the songs? Or was Will lying?

He quickly changed subject, so I made a note to myself never to bring up their creative relationship again—definitely a tender spot. But that's artists for you.

Regardless, the day had a dreamlike quality. There was

one perfect moment as we walked up lower Broadway toward the Strand Bookstore. The wind was blowing and the reddening sun was just lounging over the shorter buildings of southern Manhattan, and I realized I'd never before been enthralled in the rapture of a perfect day. I owed it to Will. For the first time in my life, I felt like an adult, but oddly free of all the obligations that supposedly came with being one.

En route back to Millbank, Will asked if I wanted to grab something to eat, and we decided on burgers at Gifford's, a small joint in Roseville, the town next to Millbank. Just outside of town, Will's cell phone rang, and he slipped the phone from his pocket and checked the caller ID.

"What up, J?"

Oh, no.

I immediately knew who it was: Jack. I was supposed to be going to his show tonight! This was bad . . . *really* bad. I checked my watch. It was already 6:30 p.m. and the show started at 7:00 p.m.. Even if I came up with a clever excuse to cut short my day with Will, I'd never make it to Jack's show in time. I'd completely blown it. As Will and Jack talked, I came up with various stories I could tell Jack, but none of them seemed viable. And then disaster struck.

"Listen, dude, I'm MIA tonight—I'm gonna grab some chow with Kat."

My heart fell to my toes. There was an obvious pause.

"Yo, Jack, you there? Jack?" Will looked over to me. "Must've lost him—he'll be cool about it."

Then his phone started buzzing again. I braced myself for the worst—the two of them figuring out I was hanging out with both them (what was I becoming?!), but when Will looked at the caller ID, his face drained. He was obviously upset.

Did Jack send him a text?

He answered rather briskly: "Yeah?"

The conversation that ensued was brief, but in those two or three minutes of mostly one-sentence responses, it escalated from "No" to "I can't right now" to "Can I do it after?"

Was he talking to Gretchen?

It was impossible to say, because the howl of the engine drowned out any sound below seventy decibels. In the end, Will hung up with a terse "Fine" and glanced my way.

I had the sinking feeling that our day was coming to an end.

"Sorry, but I have to go to my dad's shop."

"No worries," I answered. "Do you want to skip?"

"No," he said. "It'll take a minute."

Will turned off the highway and headed toward Roseville. It was what you'd call a working-class town, I suppose—the yards were smaller, American cars trumped European—and their football team had a habit of mauling ours every year when we faced off. The score last year was 55–0. It was hardly foreign soil for me because my mother always went to the Roseville Costco (other than her Ann Taylor binge, she was actually quite thrifty), and there was a broad selection of big chain stores like Bed Bath & Beyond and Target that Millbank just didn't have.

On the edge of town, Will slowed and pulled into a gas station cum auto-body repair shop. "I'll just be a minute," he said, hopping out of the car.

A few minutes passed, and as I waited, I realized Will had never even mentioned his father to me. I knew only that he lived alone with his mom in a small house over in the Fairlawn section of town. When Will walked out from the garage seconds later, he was flanked by a tall, burly man who looked like he'd spent his entire life working—and not in an office, mind you. *That's Will's dad?* His hair was greased straight back, and his hands were large and rugged.

They both walked directly to my side of the car.

"Hi," I said. "I'm Kate."

"I'm Will's father," he said in a soft-spoken voice that caught me by surprise.

"Satisfied?" Will said rudely, walking around to the driver's side of the car.

"My son doesn't like to bring his friends around— Dad doesn't strike the right note, if you know what I mean."

I just nodded, a little thrown by the palpable tension between the two.

"The principal called me, so I wanted to see what was worth skipping school over," he said, looking at his son, who was now sitting next to me and staring straight ahead.

"Oh," I responded as the air shot from my lungs. "I've never done this before, I swear."

"I'm sure you haven't, but Will here likes to be a bad boy, like his old man."

"Can we go now?" Will asked through his teeth.

"Your mother is expecting you—no detours," his dad said, and then slapped the back of the car with two quick strokes. Will quickly fired the engine and took off down Woodmont Avenue.

We didn't speak for a few minutes. Anger overflowed from his eyes, and if I were a betting girl, I'd say he was holding back tears. I didn't want to say anything to embarrass him further, but on the other hand, all of us have been there when a parent just makes us look and feel like crap in front of our friends. I had empathy galore, but how to broach the subject with him, I did not know. Mercifully, he broke the ice at a stoplight.

"He left us when I was seven," Will said. "He hates me because I hate him."

"That's brutal," I said. "You never talk about him."

"He isn't worthy."

I nodded, not ever expecting to be tied into such an intimate moment with Will.

"With that friggin' neo-Nazi, fifties greaser hair—who'd want to introduce him to anybody?"

It wasn't a pretty thing to say. Let's face it, we all have aunts and uncles and cousins who don't dress or live or act the way we want them to, but it doesn't mean they're bad people. Maybe his dad was an ass (though it appeared he was at least a concerned one), but his hair and his clothes and his job didn't seem to be the problem.

"Introducing one's parent in general is always like war of the worlds."

He nodded, like he knew what I meant. I'd seen Will's mom from afar once—she sold real estate in town—and she was petite, blond, and wore preppy clothes. My mother told me that she had come from an old-line WASP family in Greenfield that had once been wealthy (but subsequently fell on hard times), and in my mind's eye, I could see her as a young woman running off with Will's dad and causing quite a stir among the royalty of Greenfield.

"Don't tell anyone that you met him, okay?" Will said low without looking at me as we crested a hill.

I glanced over at him and nodded—not really understanding his shame, but knowing it was a secret that would stay between us.

* * *

Gifford's was busy, and a handful of MHS students sat at the counter, but we snagged a booth by the window and munched down on cheeseburgers, fries, and black-and-white milk shakes. Simply to die for.

"So when do your parents have their interview with the committee?" Will asked.

By the end of the evening, the episode with his father was forgotten, and our conversation had rambled over to the Millbank Country Club.

"Week after next, I think," I replied. "My mother— God—she's like frothing at the bit to get in."

Will chuckled and took a sip of his soda.

"And you? What do you think of it?"

"I don't really care either way. I mean, it doesn't affect me. I'm leaving for college in what, four months?"

He nodded.

"But maybe I'm wrong," I continued, not wanting to seem too anti-anything Will was part of. "The summers could be cool."

"I don't think so," he said, not looking up. "It's sort of tired."

"Really? Isn't it basically the Proud Crowd's meeting lodge?"

I meant it as a joke, but he frowned.

"They're all ridiculous."

"But they're your friends," I pointed out delicately. "I

mean, that's your scene. You and Gretchen—you're on the top of the food chain."

"Maybe it looks that way from the outside . . ." He trailed off and shifted in his seat. "Do you ever feel like you've outgrown people?"

I'd never felt that way until Dev pulled her stunt earlier in the week, but I now knew exactly what he meant. "Yeah, I kind of feel that way about high school in general."

"The Proud Crowd thing—it makes me a little ill to even think I hang with people who refer to themselves like that."

I laughed out loud. "I know, it's kind of pathetic when you think about it."

"But you'd be part of it, if you could, right?" He asked it in a strange way—almost as if it were posed to me, but also to himself. We were silent, because I think we both knew he was right. But if he knew how pathetic I'd acted over the past three weeks in a vain attempt to climb the Millbank Market, I think he would have left me right there in Gifford's with my half-eaten burger and shake.

"Lately I've been trying to avoid that crowd," he added, his eyes now meeting mine. "I'm tired of Gretchen and her minions."

But like some evil spirit that you summon merely by saying her name, none other than Gretchen Tanner herself walked into Gifford's. I couldn't freakin' believe it. With

Jodi Letz and Elisa Estrada in tow, it took all of ten seconds for Gretchen to notice us by the window. Jodi and Elisa fell into close whispering, but Gretchen appeared unfazed and tilted her head to the side, as if in thought. I glanced over at Will, who'd already noticed them as well, but if he was remotely concerned about getting discovered with yours truly, his face didn't betray even the slightest worry.

"Hey," Gretchen shouted as she walked up to the table. "You two were conspicuously missing from class this afternoon."

Econ—*great*. Up until now I'd managed to put it totally out of my head, and her reminder caused an immediate knot in my stomach.

"Bold move, Kat, and admirable for the sheer audacity." She nodded. "Should I ask where you two were?"

In Gretchen's presence, the Will of old—the Proud Crowd acolyte Will, the BMOC Will—returned like a seasoned actor who knows his cue.

"The city, hanging," he parried. "Wassup?"

Gretchen smiled thinly—well, I guess you could call it a smile. It was more like she drew the corners of her mouth toward her ears.

"Are we on for tonight?" she said, looking at Will.

Will nodded and Gretchen turned to me. "We should hang sometime."

I didn't quite know how to respond, and I managed to

get out a "Sure," but she didn't follow up with any invitation and she departed. It must've only been show for Will.

"Funny timing," Will observed, once she was out of earshot, our intimacy of minutes before now gone. "We have a project for English—that's what that was about."

"You don't owe me explanations, Will."

He blinked a few times as he registered my reaction to the whole situation.

"What's the deal with you two?" I asked.

"We're friends," he quickly answered. "I mean, we had a thing but it didn't work."

"For whom?"

He yawned nervously, trying to imply it was casual and cool. "For me."

"That explains the dagger eyes, I guess."

"I think you'd get those with or without me," he replied. "You're a threat to her."

I just squinted at him.

"C'mon, you know what I mean," he pressed with a glint in his eye.

It was like having cold water splashed in my face . . . on a really hot day.

"You don't have to say that. I know I'm not in her league."

"You're right. She's not smart enough to play in your league," he said as he leaned forward and took my hand.

This all seemed too impossible to be true. The day. Everything he was saying.

"I'm not interested in Gretchen's throne," I lied.

"Then what *do* you want?"

He couldn't have been more clear. I knew what he was asking—and offering.

KCW LLC.

MARKET RANKING: 25
TODAY'S CHANGE: ↑5

SHARE PRICE: $18.56
CHANGE: ↑6.06 (+51.7%)
L/B RATIO: 6.1
3-MONTH RANGE: $1.23 – $18.72
STATUS: PREFERRED STOCK

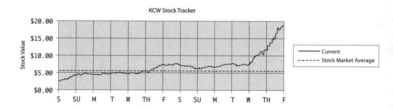

ANALYST RECOMMENDATION: Not only did this company show that it's willing to take chances in the marketplace by risking the ire of regulators, but a major player has demonstrated serious interest in this commodity. This one is about to go stratospheric.

STRONG BUY

BOOK FOUR

· · · · · · ·

AMONG THE DEN OF THIEVES

CHAPTER

18

HISTORY IS MARKED with turning points—some seen, some unseen—that represent a profound shift in the course of future events. The Boston Tea Party. The Allies invading Normandy. Bill Clinton deciding that a little one-on-one time with Monica Lewinsky would be a good idea. Surely at their inciting moments, it was unclear if these choices would result in triumph or calamity, but the decision was made nonetheless. And so it was for me after my date with Will. My righteous indignation and intrepid moralizing of just twenty-four hours previous melted away into a renewed flood of gusto and determination to rise to the top of the Market. If I needed to drive my stock price a little higher to capture Will's heart, so be it.

Was it a noble fight? Well . . . not in the Abraham

Lincoln framing of the term, but it's amazing what a little love—or at least a huge crush—will prompt you to do. C'mon! Will—for all intents and purposes—had essentially said he wanted to go out with me! Thus, my mission for the last two weeks at school now couldn't have been clearer, and within an hour of my arrival home, I'd called Dev, buried the hatchet, and was plotting how to execute the next two steps of the business plan.

My numbers got an unbelievable surge from the grandfather incident, but an even bigger boost for my stock was the revelation that I'd cut a day of school to go out with Will. Truthfully, it couldn't have been better if Dev and I had planned it. I guess it was basically a combination of co-branding and a paradigm shift—no one ever had me pegged for the type of girl to bail on school, let alone with Will—and suddenly I found myself knocking on the door to the Blue Chipdom. I was trading at eighteen dollars a share and was twenty-fifth on the Market. Dev and I spent the next week solidifying my position on the Market for the final assault on the Blue Chips, which basically consisted of me doing various small but public acts. Dev called it "raising capital." I started some cheers in the stands at the lacrosse game. I brought a case of beer that Dev snagged to Elisa Estrada's party. I even helped Nina Licht with her calc problems. As it was impossible to say who was buying in the Market, I had to cater to everyone.

Now more than ever, Dev and I were in constant communication—her texting me when opportunities presented themselves, constantly giving me directives—and everything else began to fall by the wayside. To be honest, it got to be a bit much, but I hung in there with her. Once school was over, I reasoned, I'd ride out the summer and by September I'd be at college, riding down to Poughkeepsie on the weekends to visit my boyfriend Will Bochnowski.

But not everyone was so impressed with me. The Tuesday after my date with Will, I was running out to watch the lacrosse game after school—an event that anyone who was socially conscious at Millbank would never dream of missing—when I spotted Jack at his locker, his guitar case leaning diagonally next to him. Although I'd e-mailed him a few times apologizing for missing his show, he'd never written back. In retrospect, I probably should've called him over the weekend to set the record straight, but a mix of guilt (about Will) and giddiness (about Will) had stopped me from doing the right thing.

I almost turned around to take the west exit to the field—thereby avoiding him yet again—but something forced me forward.

"Jack."

He looked my way, but when he saw who it was, his expression darkened ever so slightly. He turned back to whatever he was doing in his locker.

"How's it going?" I asked.

"Fine."

"So how was your solo show?"

"Fine."

He still wouldn't look at me. The fact that the hallway was almost entirely empty only made the situation more uncomfortable. Sometimes you want privacy for a serious convo, but sometimes it helps to have other people around to minimize the awkwardness.

"Listen," I began, "I'm sorry about missing your show."

"I heard you were out with Will. No worries."

It was clear from his delivery of "no worries" that it was anything but.

"I really wanted to be there," I offered.

Jack just nodded and said nothing.

"Can we talk about it?"

"What's to talk about?" he said directly. "Just be honest: you prefer him over me. That's totally fine."

Rational as I'd been about my friendship with Jack, face to face with what I'd done to him now, something dormant and repressed shuddered deep in my chest.

"No, it's not that," I stuttered.

"Don't lie," he snorted. "Something better came along and you took it. I just wish you'd been honest instead of playing me. 'Cause that's what you did. You played me."

"That's not fair, Jack," I pleaded.

"Get used to it." He picked up his guitar case and slung the strap over his shoulder. "I hope you're happy."

Before I could say anything, he turned and walked away. I stood there alone, watching his figure disappear, the jubilant cheers for our lacrosse team echoing softly in my ears.

When I woke up the next day, a dull, relentless ache hammered at my head, and as I dressed for school—feeling more like I was suiting up for warfare than getting ready for classes—I couldn't shake a simmering anger invading every crevice of my being. Like some borderline lunatic, I even found myself muttering furiously under my breath. It was the Market. All night I'd been awake, thinking about what had happened with Jack—about our conversation in the hallway—about how I'd bailed on him. But as much as I knew that I should just forget about the Market, to stop playing these stupid games, I couldn't. The rational voices in my head were drowned out by the all-consuming need to make it to the top.

I didn't see Dev until Econ class, and because Mr. Walsh was such a rule freak, we barely got to say hello before he started speaking. In a move of expert manipulation pulled right from the Gretchen Tanner playbook, I'd managed to smooth over my cutting class the previous week—I played the depressed-about-grandpa's-death card—but I knew I had to watch my step. That day it was Gretchen's turn to give her presentation, and Mr. Walsh gave her a little introduction. She was focusing on the 1980s, a time, Mr. Walsh said, when Wall Street was king in terms of its cultural influence. Gretchen walked a little nervously to the front of the room and shuffled her papers before beginning to speak.

"'Greed is good,'" she started. "This is the most important line of movie dialogue, in my mind, from any movie made in the eighties. In that one line, the entire mindset of the eighties, the Wall Street decade, is summed up."

I could see a bunch of kids immediately slump in their chairs, but Mr. Walsh's ears perked up. Unlike most of my classmates, I knew what movie it came from: the appropriately named *Wall Street*, directed by Oliver Stone and starring Charlie Sheen as Bud Fox and Michael Douglas as the infamous Gordon Gekko. It was a morality tale about money, friendship, and how far one should go to earn the almighty dollar. My dad made me watch it with him one summer night, and besides being drawn to a very hot and sexy younger version of Charlie Sheen (a total freak now), the story was weirdly compelling. Gretchen wove in and out of discussing the movie by ducking into real-life stories of corporate greed from the book *Den of Thieves* by James Stewart, which, intriguingly, was about Michael Milken.

(Was that a connection?) By the end, Gretchen wound down her report by recounting the final scene between Charlie Sheen and Michael Douglas when Bud Fox confronts Gordon Gekko in Central Park.

"Is greed good?" Gretchen asked to end her report. "*Wall Street* tries to tell us the moral dangers of greed, but I don't know if it is convincing—something in it tells me the moralizing champion, Charlie Sheen, isn't the real hero—Michael Douglas is."

The class broke into a lackluster round of applause. Several boys in the back row woke up and made some lame catcalls. Gretchen walked back to her seat, and a few of the Proud Crowd patted her on the back. Mr. Walsh said nothing, but I noted he did not join the class in applause. He rose from his desk, grabbed a piece of chalk, and turned to the blackboard. He wrote: IS GREED GOOD?

"How many people believe greed is good?"

A few hands went up, mostly comprised of Gretchen's friends.

"And how many think greed is bad?"

Most of the class raised their hands.

I didn't vote.

"Gretchen," Mr. Walsh said, "it appears most of the class disagrees with you—that Michael Douglas is not a hero and what he represents is not heroic. What do you have to say to them?"

Gretchen looked pained. She probably thought she'd breeze through this report like most of the class had, but she'd picked a subject that was dear to Mr. Walsh. In fact, because he left the Street and came to teach, one would suspect he wasn't on the "greed is good" side of the fight at all. He was a do-gooder by nature, and I'm sure his run on Wall Street (by all accounts a successful one) brought him face-to-face with what greed could do, even to good men and women.

"Winners win, and losers lose," she responded. "I didn't make the movie, I just watched it, and that's what I felt."

"Yeah. Don't hate the player, hate the game," some meathead chimed in from the back.

"But the ending clearly showed what Michael Douglas truly was: a cold, heartless man with a soul rotted out by greed. He's no hero, and the director clearly wanted you to believe that Charlie Sheen was the man we're meant to follow. It's about right and wrong. It's too easy to say 'hate the game, not the player.' In that world, no one's responsible for anything."

I'd long admired him for his moral high ground, but there was something about his tone that day—perhaps it was an attitude of utter certainty, his confident assurance of his moral position—that made me crazy.

I couldn't help myself.

"I actually think Gretchen is right," I jumped in.

Everyone turned toward me like I had smashed a bottle on the ground.

Mr. Walsh glanced over at me and raised an eyebrow. "Unexpected support from our little leftist."

"Just because the screenwriter tried to make Charlie Sheen the hero doesn't mean he was, no matter how you want to construe it."

A big "Oooooohhhh" erupted from the boys in the last row. Mr. Walsh turned red, and I assumed at this point he was a little angry, but I wasn't about to hedge my position. I was tired of teachers and parents trying to pretend that the world was fair and that good things happened to good people. The meek did not inherit the earth. They ended up Seventy-one on the Market—anonymous and forgotten.

"I think you're being simplistic," he said.

"That's funny—I thought you were."

Another burst of giggles and shouts filled the classroom, and as much as I knew that I needed to back down, to give up this fight that wasn't my own, I only felt emboldened. Across the room, Gretchen and her posse watched me wide-eyed and grinning, impressed by the battle I was waging.

"Why don't you explain to the class your 'complex' theory, then?" he said.

"Fine," I started. "Take Michael Douglas and Charlie Sheen—which one do you remember more from the movie, Mr. Walsh?"

He sat down on his desk. The hardened gleam disappeared from his eyes, and his thirst to skewer a student faded. "Well, I would say Douglas is the more memorable character."

"And what piece of dialogue spoken by any character in the movie is the most memorable?"

"'Greed is good,'" he said.

"By Douglas," I added. "And do you remember any single piece of dialogue spoken by your so-called hero, Charlie Sheen?"

He shook his head no.

"That's because even though he's supposed to be our moral hero, he's a wimp. The movie is supposed to be anti-greed, but all too tellingly, Douglas is the only thing we remember. Greed is our hero, our romance. Financial success, or say, in high school, popularity—at any cost—is the American dream. Its victors are heroes."

It was as if someone else had taken over my body.

"Well, that's certainly one way of looking at it," he said evenly.

"It's the real way, the American way," I sneered.

"If you—"

"No—all that nice guy stuff is bull."

"Ms. Winthrop," he breathed, "you've always been bright, but you used to also be humble."

"I could have said the same of you."

Jaws hit the floor. The class was dead silent—I don't think anyone was even breathing.

Did that really come out of my mouth?

Mr. Walsh looked at me carefully and then down at his desk.

"Why don't we discuss this further," he began as he pulled out his pen. "In detention."

Right then the bell rang. I put my books in my bag and didn't even look up at Mr. Walsh as I exited the room and headed to my locker. I was wrong to be so harsh, but something about finally saying something back to a teacher, even a great one like Mr. Walsh, felt right.

"Kat!"

I slammed my last book into my locker and turned around to discover Gretchen and her crew walking up behind me. She was smiling, clearly amused by my standing up for her paper.

"Thanks—for today in class."

"No worries, you were right," I said, trying to impart that it wasn't for her that I stood up to him. As I looked Gretchen in the eyes, I suddenly wondered if part of the reason I'd gone after Mr. Walsh so hard wasn't simply to impress her. Had I somehow internalized Step Five of Dev's plan—"a merger with Gretchen Tanner"? Was that what had made me go so overboard?

"Listen," Gretchen said. "I'm having some people over tonight—you should come."

"I've got plans," I said. I'm not sure how I pulled it off, but I managed to be nonchalant about her advances. It helped that I wasn't lying. The week before, Dev and I had made a date to sack out at her house and rent old John Hughes movies—you know, *The Breakfast Club* and *Sixteen Candles*. "But thanks for the offer."

Gretchen touched my arm.

"C'mon, Will's going to be there," she pressed.

Yeah, she wasn't the Queen Bee for nothing. The fact that Gretchen implied there was something between Will and me made my pulse race, and despite my better judgment, I found myself getting drawn into her vortex. Could I legitimately pass up a chance to spend an evening with Gretchen and her crew, if our plan was to work?

It was right then that Dev spotted us across the hall and scurried right up between Gretchen and me.

"Weren't you Miss Ballsy today," she said.

Right away I saw what she was up to; she was trying to capitalize on the whole Walsh episode to make me appear cooler than I was—a rebel questioning authority. I looked at her sharply, trying to silently communicate that she needed to stay away from this situation.

"So are we still on for tonight?" Dev asked, clearly not getting my communiqué.

Out of the corner of my eyes, I could feel Gretchen look at me in mocking disbelief, as if to say—*She's why you were turning us down?*

"Huh?" I grunted in the poorest of concealed non-answers.

"Movie night?" Dev prompted.

Behind her, Jodi and Carrie smirked at each other and then rolled their eyes.

I mean, if she was trying to puff me up in front of Gretchen, revealing that I spent my Friday nights watching movies at home wasn't a well thought out idea. It didn't occur to me that perhaps, subconsciously, Dev didn't want me to fall under Gretchen's spell.

I realized then that this was a decisive moment—not a personal choice, but a business decision. I struggled to distance myself from the situation . . . to look at it objectively . . . but with Gretchen and her friends surrounding me, and dreams of blue-chip status swirling in my head, my deductive skills were clumsy and imprecise. Wouldn't being seen hanging out with Gretchen and the Proud Crowd send my Market number skyrocketing?

Of course it would.

I knew immediately what I had to do—and if Dev had the full picture of what was unfolding, she would've told me to do the same thing. I know it. If I passed on Gretchen and the Proud Crowd now, our plan would fail. This was my big chance to both merge with Gretchen and create that little bit of alchemy every great plan needs to succeed. Dev would just have to sit tight until I could fill her in later on what I was doing.

"Actually, I'm hanging with Gretchen tonight," I replied.

Gretchen's head snapped back, and her eyelids lowered ever so slightly—a pleased smile on her face.

"Come again?" Dev said.

"Yeah," I continued, now settling comfortably into my role, "she's having a party—Will's going to be there."

Dev just stared at me, clearly unwilling to accept what she was hearing.

"We had plans," she hissed through clenched teeth.

"Movie night?" Carrie Bell asked with a little mocking laugh.

"Puh-lease," Jodi seconded, apparently tasting blood in the water. "So you could make hot chocolate and knit friendship bracelets?"

The girls all laughed—their snickers like little knives—and Dev's cheeks burned red. I tried winking to let her know what I was up to, but she was clueless. Momentarily, I debated coming to her defense, suggesting that she come too, but that would've only ruined things. No, I had to hold firm, no matter how horrible it was to see Dev twisting in the wind. Besides, she *had* to understand the hand I was playing. There were always losses accumulated during an M&A—movie night would be one of them.

"Kat's ready to play with the big girls now," Gretchen drawled after a moment, and she slipped her arm through mine. "Aren't you Kit-Kat?"

I looked over at her, and Gretchen stared at me, apparently waiting for me to affirm what she'd just said. It was that classic moment in any initiation when you had to show your allegiance to the new order—be it the Mafia, the military, or the Proud Crowd. Awful as it was, I swallowed and took a deep breath.

"Yeah, I am."

"I see," Dev whispered. "I see."

Her face was inscrutable as she turned and walked away. As she did, Gretchen and the girls drew closer—whispering and smiling—and our bodies formed a circle, blocking out everyone else. For a second, I thought Dev might turn and give me a knowing wink, but she just disappeared into the sea of other students flowing down the hallway.

CHAPTER

19

THE DOOR SWUNG open and Gretchen handed me a glass of bubbling champagne.

"What's this for?"

"We're celebrating." She grinned.

Through all of detention and my whole drive over to Gretchen's house I tried to imagine what the evening would hold, and this was certainly never how I'd imagined it beginning. Not three and a half weeks before, I was practically ridiculed off the property, and now here I was being welcomed with open arms.

I took the glass and Gretchen motioned for me to follow her back through the house. Her parents didn't seem to be home, and except for the low rumble of a techno beat thumping from a room somewhere in the house, there were no signs of life. As we snaked our way through the darkened spaces, the music gradually grew louder until finally we arrived in a large open room that overlooked the tennis court. Candles, burning smoky and red, peppered the surfaces, and once my eyes adjusted to the dim, flickering light, I discovered Elisa, Jodi, and Carrie—champagne flutes in hand—lounging casually on silk pillows on the floor. It seemed we were in a game room of sorts—a shuffleboard table lined one wall, a pool table stood unused at the far end, and MTV played silently on the largest flat-screen television I'd ever seen.

The girls nodded to me, and Gretchen picked up a bottle of Veuve Clicquot from a felt-covered table and passed it around for everyone to refill their glasses.

"Take a seat," she said as she gestured toward an open space.

"What are we celebrating?" I asked. Gretchen looked at Elisa, who giggled and sipped her drink. Jodi pursed her lips and studied her shoes, which I estimated at three hundred plus.

"You," Carrie said.

"To Kat," Gretchen announced, holding her champagne up. "Better late than never."

They all laughed, and I couldn't help but join them. I took a seat on the floor next to Elisa and sipped the champagne. I wasn't much of a drinker, but I could handle a glass of champagne . . . or two. I drank it slowly, and gradually I merged into the scene.

Decadent as the night was—raiding Gretchen's mother's closet and trying on all her Harry Winston jewelry, opening more bottles of champagne, and taking a quick dip in the bubbling hot tub—fundamentally, it wasn't any different from a hundred other nights Dev, Callie, and I had spent together. We talked about boys, and then we talked about boys some more. We did some catty chatting about girls, the ones we hated and the underclassmen we admired, and we talked about Walsh and the other teachers. We talked about how annoying our moms were, and how much we were going to miss them once we got to college. We talked about going to college and never coming back to Millbank, though we all knew that was a lie and that we would see each other at the homecoming game next fall.

As I sat there, I have to admit there were moments when the whole scene made me a little melancholy. A quiet part of me missed my true friends, and I wondered what Dev was doing right then. I'd tried to call her the moment I got in my car after detention, but her cell went straight to voice mail. I'd tried again at home, but still straight to voice mail. By dinnertime, I started to worry that perhaps the two of us weren't on the same page about the M&A of Gretchen and her crew, but I told myself that, given the circumstances, I should just put the whole situation in the back of my mind until we could clear the air, if it needed clearing.

But maybe I should try her one more time . . .

The doorbell snapped me out of my worrying, and when my eyes looked down the long hallway that separated the game room from the front of the house, I could see Will's blue eyes glowing. By his side were two of his band members, Dee Brown and Walter Pond . . . and Jack.

Oh no.

As the boys sauntered into the family room, Will looked directly at me. There was definitely an element of surprise written on his face, and while Gretchen had told me that Will was coming, it was now clear she hadn't informed Will that I would be here. Jack wouldn't even meet my gaze, and it was also clear that he was holding to the same tactic he used when he saw me at the BookStop: pretend I wasn't there.

While Jack awkwardly went over and looked through Gretchen's DVDs, Will effortlessly joined the party and pecked all the girls on the cheek. When he got to me, he simply said, "Hey," and sat down next to me on the couch. Once the conversation started up, he turned to me and whispered, "Meet me on the porch out back," and a moment later, he got up and announced he had to make a call. He walked out of the room like he knew the place intimately, and it unexpectedly stirred a little pang of jealousy. I quickly remembered, however, who he had just asked to meet for a rendezvous.

I waited a good five minutes before excusing myself, eventually asking where the powder room was located. There were two, one by the foyer and the other just off the kitchen, and I quickly deduced that Will had known this and thus suggested the back porch, which was accessible from the kitchen only.

Through the darkness, I could see a cigarette ember glowing outside. I quietly slid open the glass door and moved toward Will, who was silhouetted in the moonlight.

"Can you see me?" I joked, half hoping he'd remember the words he spoke to me the first night.

"I have to admit something to you," he said, staring off into the dark.

"Go ahead," I whispered, half of me scared to listen and the other half thrilled with anticipation.

"Those were Jack's words—that first night."

It was like a little jab to my belly. The eight words that changed my life—"You were always the one I couldn't see"—were falsely spoken. Will had stolen them from Jack Clayton.

"Why are you telling me that?" The tone of my voice was more cross than I had intended, but Will was unfazed.

"Because they were his words and you were his observation, but I've been falling for you ever since."

That line was more than a jab—it was a full body shot.

"Falling is a slippery word," I warned. Perhaps he feared

that Jack would sell him out, or perhaps it was just a simple desire to come clean; either way I appreciated the honesty. "I guess we all play parts we haven't written."

"Yeah, but I don't want to play a part with you—that's why I'm telling you." He turned and tossed his cigarette off the porch before cupping my face in his hands. He kissed me on the lips once, and hard. "Don't trust her," he breathed into my ear.

"Who?"

"Gretchen," he whispered. "She doesn't want you to succeed."

"Succeed at what?"

He was very quiet for a few moments, like he was considering his words carefully. "I meant us," he finally said. "She doesn't want us to succeed."

"I don't care what she thinks."

"Good," he breathed. And he kissed me again.

Just then the light in the kitchen popped on, and the porch light followed shortly thereafter. We quickly separated, and by the time the sliding glass door opened, revealing Gretchen flanked by Jodi, we were on opposite sides of the porch and Will had managed to light another cigarette.

"You two can't get enough of each other," Gretchen said. "It's so cute."

I fidgeted nervously and I heard Will exhale loudly, like he was letting go of a little anxiety.

"Will," Gretchen continued. "I'm glad you're here because I had something important to share with Kat."

Will turned toward Gretchen with suspicion in his eyes, and for a second I could swear he was terrified of what she might say. I looked down at my shoes, almost feeling like I had interrupted her and Will, and not the other way around.

Was Gretchen about to call me out?

"It's about the Black & White," she said like she was singing a song. "I'm putting Kat at my table!"

I couldn't believe it—I was speechless.

"But there's no room for her," Jodi complained. "The table's totally full."

Clearly, Jodi hadn't reconciled herself to my newfound status and still had it out for me.

Gretchen shrugged her shoulders with nonchalance. "Well, you wouldn't mind sitting at Jack's table, right?"

"What?"

"Kat can have your seat."

If I hadn't known how cruel Jodi was, I might have felt sorry for her. Betrayed by the girl who was no doubt her idol, she looked destroyed.

"Well, if that's what you want," she mumbled pathetically.

"Perfect," Gretchen concluded before turning back to me. "What do you say?"

I walked over and threw my arms around her and gave her a light kiss on the cheek. "Thank you! Thank you!"

"It's nothing, really."

Listlessly, Jodi wandered back inside, and Will just stood there, mute. His eyes were telling me he didn't trust a word Gretchen was saying, but I was too thrilled to care. Finally, as if nothing had been said of any interest to him, he mumbled that he had to take off.

Making his exit, he gave Gretchen a little kiss on the cheek and then turned to me with a weak smile. "You keep falling up." And with a wink, he left.

An hour or so later, Gretchen followed me to the front door. It was past my curfew for a school night, but when I'd called my mother and told her where I was, naturally she said it was fine. Standing on the front steps now, I looked up at the stars. They were blazing in a way that you rarely see under the canopy of the suburban lights.

"Beautiful night," I said.

"Yes," Gretchen answered. "Thanks for coming."

"I'll see you tomorrow," I said. "And thanks again for the Black & White."

"It's nothing."

Not that I had been on many by then, but strangely, it felt like the end of a date—like Gretchen and I had passed a threshold. I waved and made my way to my car. As I looked over my shoulder back up at her house, I pictured Will kissing me on the porch, and it made my heart flutter to even think about it. Gretchen stood at the door, smiling, and she kept the light on until I started the engine. Finally she nodded and went back in to her small party that I suspected would go on late into the night.

As I crept slowly down the steep hill, I could feel my tires slipping on the gravel.

KCW LLC.

MARKET RANKING: 19
TODAY'S CHANGE: ↑5

SHARE PRICE: $29.16
　　　CHANGE: ↑10.06 (+43%)
L/B RATIO: 9.7
3-MONTH RANGE: $1.23 – $30.13
STATUS: BLUE CHIP

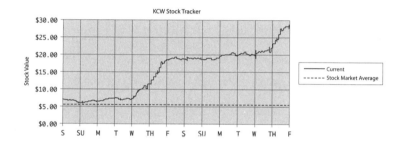

ANALYST RECOMMENDATION: A merger with GRT? Could it get any better for this stock? This CEO is making all the right moves.

STRONG BUY

· ·

CHAPTER

20

Had I turned to the Dark Side?

I'd be lying if I didn't admit that I enjoyed hanging out with Gretchen and the Proud Crowd, but that didn't mean I was going to become one of her brainless clones. No way. In the light of day, I took the party for what it was: an unexpected entry to the Black & White and an opportunity to deepen my relationship with Will. Dev would have been proud of my cold-hearted approach to Gretchen. Machiavellian? Mata Hari-esque? Perhaps. But by this point I was savvy enough to know that the key to climbing to the top of the Market was keeping Gretchen close enough to add luster to my shares, but far enough away that I could shine on my own.

When I woke up and checked the Market the next

morning—there it was: I was officially . . . a Blue Chip!! Granted, ranked at number 19, I'd just barely cracked it, but I was certified nonetheless. I could barely restrain myself from doing a little victory dance as I snatched my phone from the cradle and called Dev. When she answered, I launched right in.

"Did you see? We did it!" I yelled. "I'm a Blue Chip!"

Right when I was expecting Dev to be at her giddiest, there was dead silence on the other end of the line.

"Hello?"

"I'm here," she said. "How could you?"

"How could I what?"

"Don't play dumb," she snapped. "You totally humiliated me in front of Gretchen."

"Dev, I left you messages last night to explain, but you never called me back. I was doing it for the Market—for the final step of your business plan—and it totally worked! They were practically eating out of my hand last night."

"You're full of it. You walked all over me to get what you wanted."

"Why are you overreacting?"

"Overreacting?!"

"You're not listening to me," I cried as I felt things spiraling out of control. "It was just business—part of your plan. *Really*. It was that moment of alchemy you went on and on about. It's not a big deal."

"Not a big deal? Not a big deal?" her voice quivered. "You were a total bitch to me. And maybe, just maybe, it really was a step in the plan, but even if it was, it was still wrong. You got greedy. It was completely out of line."

So many thoughts collided in my head at once—the fact that she'd been driving me crazy with the Market, how it was seemingly okay for her to pop things on me out of the blue, like Princeton guy, but when I did it, it was wrong— that my mouth froze. I may not have been entirely in the right, but she wasn't exactly innocent either.

But before I could apologize, Dev launched back in.

"You're so full of it, it's disgusting," she said. "You ditched me so you could be one of them, plain and simple."

"But—"

"Since you're apparently too good for me now, do me a favor. Don't ever call me again!" She hung up on me.

I was so upset that it took every ounce of self-control not to hurl the phone against the wall and watch it shatter into a hundred pieces, so instead I slammed it down into my comforter. I walked over to my computer and refreshed the Market, my obsession apparently uninhibited by my falling out with Dev.

In one twenty-four-hour period, my life and my dreams became one, and together they were one big nightmare. As I watched my Market ranking jump from nineteen to sixteen in less time than it took Dev and me to implode, I wondered how I'd save our friendship. I fell onto my bed and buried my head in my pillows as my chest shuddered with deep, painful sobs. For what or who, I couldn't exactly tell you, but I knew somehow it was all shackled to the Market.

With Gretchen's tacit stamp of approval and (for those in the know) my newly minted Blue Chip status, my life was transformed overnight. Suddenly Gretchen was extending invitations to go swimming at the Millbank Country Club, and I was even offered my very own seat at the Proud Crowd table in the cafeteria. In a lot of ways, it was still pretty baffling, but I wasn't complaining. With less than two weeks left of high school, the world was my proverbial oyster *(why hadn't this happened sooner?),* and life took on an almost surreal quality: my walk more confident, my smile more seductive. Every day there was somewhere to be—trips to the mall with Elisa, late-night convos with Nina, a private party at Café Electric—and I reveled in this new, though foreign, life. I'd become someone new, someone sought after. In many ways, it made me think back to that afternoon when Dev and I hatched our plan, and we pored over pictures of girls Dev referred to as Latebloomers. Suddenly, I was that girl, and I was reaping all the rewards. Glamorous as my life was on the surface, however, I was feeling torn apart inside—torn apart by what had happened with Dev.

A week after that fateful day, I took a gamble that Callie might be working at Bella's, and I turned down River Road. Sure enough, when I walked in, Callie was on break, sitting in the back room reading a stack of magazines and sipping an espresso.

"Hey," I said as I gave her a smooch on the cheek and plopped down in the chair opposite.

"Where've you been?" she asked.

"You know."

"Mmm-hmmm, too busy for Cal," she observed, and looked back down at her magazine.

"I know, I'm sorry."

Callie fixed me with a stare before dropping her magazine on the table. I noticed she didn't have that bouncy smile I so loved. "Kate, when are you going to get tired of this game?"

"What do you mean? What game?"

"A month ago you came to me with a sob story about being Number Seventy-one, about being a 'nobody.' And I warned you not to care what other people thought, but you and Dev had a plan, so I played along because you said you needed me. And now you don't seem to need anyone."

"What are you talking about?"

"You haven't been to a brunch with Dev and me in two weeks, you bailed on helping me with the graduation decorations, and you haven't called once in over a week."

"I've been—"

"So you come in here with the 'you know' excuse?" she finished without missing a beat. "And it's not just me—now you and Dev are in this huge fight."

"She told you about that?"

"Of course she did."

"You have to help me. She won't talk to me. She either doesn't take my calls, or when I go up to her in person she just walks away."

Callie shook her head, obviously concerned.

"I don't want to say it, but I told you so."

I was silent for a moment, desperately wanting a confidante.

"Can I tell you something?" I asked.

She raised an eyebrow and cocked her head.

"Do you ever think the reason why Dev's all upset is because she's not getting to be the Latebloomer? Because she's still stuck where she is?"

Callie's face was like concrete. I'm not sure she was convinced of my analysis of Dev. After a few moments of silence, she sighed.

"Free pass," she said. "I'm giving you a free pass."

"What for?"

"You're all kinds of twisted around—you don't even know who your real friends are," Callie continued. "The three of us need to sit down—you, me, and Dev, no excuses—

because, to be honest, you've both been whack ever since this stupid Market thing started, and we need to fix it."

I studied her for a few moments and then glanced out the window. A tractor trailer filled with brand-new BMWs rumbled by beneath a sky pink-hued from the setting sun. I wondered then, darkly and only for a fleeting instant, if my friendship with Dev had come and gone.

"This Saturday," she declared. "Are we on?"

The morning of the Black & White?

"I don't know," I said.

"What do you mean?" Callie snapped. "Don't you want things to go back to how they used to be?"

I looked at her and shrugged my shoulders and said, "Yes." It was true. I definitely wanted to reconcile with Dev—I couldn't imagine my life without her—but did I want to go back to being Seventy-one? Did I want to go back to movie night every Friday? Or did I want Will and the Black & White and parties at Gretchen's?

Why couldn't I have both?

CHAPTER

21

THAT NIGHT WAS the big moment, the main event, the evening to end all evenings—for my mother.

"Where have you been?" she fumed, rollers in her hair, an eyelash curler clutched in her hand, when I cruised into the house fresh from a spruce-up at Images (I needed something to make me feel better after my convo with Callie). "We're supposed to meet the Tanners at the club in thirty minutes!"

Yes, it was time for my parents' all-important one-on-one meeting with the Tanners. Strictly speaking, this was not the final step in their application process, but as Abby Tanner was chairwoman of the New Membership Committee, it was well known that if she approved of the applicant, it was basically a done deal. Hence the fate-of-the-world-hangs-in-the-balance level of anxiety for my mom.

"Don't stress. I'll be ready before Dad."

And this was true, too. If we had to be anywhere by a certain time, Dad would inevitably snooze away on the couch in his study until fifteen minutes before we were supposed to leave, while my mother fluttered about, admonishing him to get ready, until it escalated into a full-blown diplomatic crisis. It was a routine I'd witnessed a thousand times. He'd wander into the hall, they'd bicker, and he'd shave and prep while the hemming and hawing continued until finally they got out the door, only to discover a smear of white shaving cream hanging off his ear that, at that very instant, would drip down and stain his shirt. At that point, there'd be either a family laugh . . . or a family breakdown. One time, my mother walked back into the house and refused to come out, but more often than not, it ended in laughter. It was no accident that my parents had been married as long as they had. Yes, they got into it from time to time, but at the end of it all, they worked well together.

I hoped I would be so lucky one day.

"No, you won't," I heard my father yell, as he suddenly appeared in the hallway, the back of his hair disheveled, no doubt from the pillow he was napping on. Nothing got Dad going like a little competition, and I watched him hurry into the bathroom and heard the spigots squeak on. He barked out an outfit request to my mom.

With my hair and nails already done, all I had to do was slip into my dress—an appropriately conservative Ralph Lauren scoop-neck number—and grab some jewelry, so I knew there was no way he was going to beat me. It took me all of two minutes and thirty-eight seconds, and after zipping down the stairs, I ended up beating Dad by more than three minutes.

When he did sheepishly arrive, however—thankfully, because my mother was wearing out the new linoleum floor with her pacing—disaster had struck. A steady stream of blood was inching down his chin. This was cause for alarm, because whenever Dad cut himself shaving, it was like he'd opened an artery. He's what you'd call a real bleeder.

"Frank! Didn't I tell you to shave last night?" she started.

Mom was always encouraging Dad to shave the day before a big meeting or event because his face was so sensitive, but like most middle-aged men (or so I've observed with my friends' fathers) he never paid any attention to her warnings.

My dad grumbled something inaudible, and she expertly pulled a Kleenex from the box on the counter, ripped a corner off, and pressed it to the open wound. After a few minutes, the tissue shred just stayed on by itself, the blood acting as an adhesive.

"Let's go. It'll stop by the time we get there," Mom announced like a general about to take the field of battle. "At least it better."

And with that, we were off.

Cute Snobby Guy who ran the front desk at the club showed us into the private dining room behind the library. Minutes before in the parking lot, Mom had pulled the Kleenex from my father's face, and much to our relief, his chin seemed to be holding up.

As I circled around the wood-paneled room, I counted six place settings at the table, and I silently wondered who the sixth person was who would be joining us.

"Kat, do you and your parents want anything while you're waiting?" Cute Snobby Guy offered.

Out of the corner of my eye, I saw my mother look over at me, confused.

After coming to the club a bunch of times with the Proud Crowd, I'd actually gotten to know Cute Snobby Guy (his name was Max, in fact). Elisa admitted to me that she had a huge crush on him, but while all the girls agreed he was a total cutie, I'd been informed there was an unspoken rule of no smooching the staff, Will being the exception of course. . . .

"We're fine, Max, thanks."

Max nodded officially and turned to leave, and just as

he got to the door, in walked the Tanners. I'd never met Abby Tanner before, but I'd certainly seen her on television. Here was the crazy thing: she was more beautiful in person. Long brown hair that was naturally wavy, and blue eyes flecked with violet—she looked like Elizabeth Taylor in her prime. For his part, Mr. Tanner appeared even bigger than in his portrait, and his slow gait and easy drawl suggested a Texan replanted in the soil of Jersey. My mom had once described him as a tall drink of water (I have no idea where she'd seen him, in town?), and now I grasped what she meant. He was graceful and manly. Each step flowed continuously into the next until he was upon you, and then you felt like you were swimming in emerald ponds.

After the usual greetings, and nice-to-meet-you's, Mrs. Tanner squinted and then gestured at my father's chin.

"What happened there?"

I shot a look over at my mom, and no joke, I thought she might split in half and transform—like a werewolf, or the Incredible Hulk—into some crazy beast. Whether she'd eat Mrs. Tanner for obnoxiously pointing out my father's chin, or Dad himself for not shaving a day in advance, I just couldn't quite tell.

"Razor," Dad answered with a bashful smile.

Mr. Tanner stepped up and put a firm hand on my dad's back. "Happens to me all the time."

That was cool, I thought to myself.

"Kit-Kat," I heard a familiar call from the doorway, and from the nickname, I knew right away who it was.

Gretchen.

"Hey!"

She was wearing a sexy, empire-waist dress with diamond drop earrings, and yet again, she proved herself to be the most gorgeous person in the room. Gretchen came over and gave me a big hug, and for the second time in two minutes, I noticed my mother's head jerk in my direction. I guess she was wondering how it was that I suddenly knew everyone so well.

"When my parents said they were having dinner with your family, I just had to come," Gretchen explained before going on to introduce herself to my parents. Beaming, my mother shook her hand.

"It's always nice to meet one of Kate's friends," my mother gushed as Mrs. Tanner looked on.

"She's the best," Gretchen answered.

I have to admit, I was somewhat perplexed by her appearance, but I just smiled. Mrs. Tanner delicately took a glass of wine from the full tray a waiter had just delivered. "So you're a senior as well, Kate. And where are you off to next fall?"

"Brown."

"Very impressive." She swiveled her head toward Gretchen and nodded. "We always thought Gretchen was going to go to an Ivy League school, but she proved us wrong."

A brief silence filled the room, and my father cleared his throat uncomfortably. Gretchen, the master of poise, appeared unfazed by her mother's slam, but I had to imagine that part of her was shriveling up inside. Hard as it is to believe, I felt bad for her.

"Well, there are so many good schools," my mother interjected.

"Definitely," my father chimed.

Mrs. Tanner just tapped her perfectly manicured nail against her glass and stared at her daughter with barely veiled disappointment.

"That's enough, Ab," Mr. Tanner said in a low voice before turning to my parents and smiling. "Shall we sit down and order?"

Desperate for a safe exit from this outrageously awkward exchange, we all nodded eagerly and moved toward the table.

As it turned out, my parents really got along with the Tanners. I wouldn't say that they were on their way to sending each other Christmas cards and going on family vacations, but the conversation flowed easily, and when my mom and Mrs. Tanner discovered they both had a passion for antiquing in Bucks County, they were off to the races. Dad even got in on the lovefest, because Mr. Tanner started talking football (seems he was a Texas Longhorn guy), and like most men, my dad could shoot the bull ad infinitum about anything sports related. They jawed on about running backs and the BCS, and before I knew it they were making plans to play golf together.

"Looks like it's going well," I whispered to Gretchen.

She grinned slyly and nodded. "I gave your family good pre-rap. Just remember who had your back."

It was textbook Gretchen: simultaneously ingratiating herself, but also letting you know that she was the string-puller, the playmaker, the Svengali behind the scenes. And what was given could also be taken away.

Despite the fact that I constantly had to be on my guard around her, it was actually great that Gretchen had come, because we all know how boring it is to have to sit through a long dinner with your parents and another couple. Sure, I needed to be there to say my lines whenever the Tanners had a question about MHS or college, but for the most part, Gretchen and I were able just to chat between ourselves, and there were few people as entertaining as she.

"Meanwhile, I had the best idea last night," she whispered.

"What?"

"You know how I usually have a party after graduation every year? Well this year I was thinking maybe you wanted to do it at your house. I'll help you plan it."

"Really?"

I was shocked. Gretchen's party had become an annual event since we were freshman—and from what I'd been told, it made that little shindig I went to last month look like a middle-school cookie party.

"But that's your night."

She shook her head. "I totally wouldn't care if you did it. Besides, it would be so much fun for us to do together. The whole school would come. We could call it 'Heaven'—you know, 'cause the 'Hell' of high school is over?"

A huge party? At my house? I wasn't so sure that my parents would be into it—I could just picture my dad's reaction when he found one of the football players booting in our bathroom. But wouldn't it be so cool to throw the final party of senior year? Wouldn't that once and for all cement my position as this year's Latebloomer? The ultimate coup de grace over my sister's previously superior reputation?

But another question flew into my mind: why was Gretchen offering to do this? Was there an agenda behind it?

"I don't think my parents would be into it."

She leaned forward. "Watch and learn."

I realized what she was going to do before she even opened her mouth.

"Mrs. Winthrop," she cooed as she inserted herself into

our parents' conversation, "Kate and I were talking and we just had a terrific idea. We want to plan a graduation-night party together. Would you and Mr. Winthrop be okay if we had it at your house?"

I'll give her this; it was a masterful move. There was no way my mother could say no. I'm sure the idea of Gretchen Tanner and her daughter cohosting a party together was right up there with me marrying a prince, anyway, but even if my mother had wanted to refuse, there was no way she could in front of Mr. and Mrs. Tanner. Not with club membership on the line.

And neither could I.

My father wrinkled his brow, but my mother jumped in before he could say anything. "That sounds wonderful. Assuming of course that Abby and Bill are okay with it."

The Tanners nodded.

"I'll give you my caterer's number," Mrs. Tanner reassured my mother. "And a good party rental person, so it's not too much work for you. Just ring me tomorrow."

While my father was surely calculating how much this party was going to cost him, my mother's eyes glimmered with excitement. No doubt she couldn't wait to call Mrs. Tanner.

"See?" Gretchen said as our parents fell back into their own conversation.

"I'm impressed."

She took a sip of her mineral water before touching my knee. "So, you have to tell me. What's the deal with you and Will?"

That was out of left field.

"What do you mean?"

"You have been spending a ton of time together. Are you guys hooking up?"

In the Tanner-Winthrop merger, Will Bochnowski was the one deal point that had never been closed. No matter what she claimed, I suspected she still had a thing for him, and I knew this was a subject that needed to be handled with extreme caution. Like a vial of nitroglycerine, one fumble and the whole thing would blow up in my face.

"I can never tell what guys are thinking," I answered.

Gretchen reached across the table and grabbed a roll from the basket. "That's not what I asked," she pressed. "Are you guys hooking up?"

Thankfully, before I could answer, Mrs. Tanner put her hand on Gretchen's arm. "You're not having more bread, are you?"

Gretchen's tongue darted across her teeth. She put the roll down. "Of course not."

"That's what I thought." Mrs. Tanner nodded, turned back to my mother, and picked right back up with their conversation.

Gretchen said nothing for a few moments, and I picked

my purse up from the floor and feigned looking for something to spare her the extra humiliation.

It was pretty disturbing to see Gretchen interact with her parents. Although my relationship with my family could be a little bonkers sometimes, I never doubted the fact that they loved me. Look, I'm not saying Mrs. Tanner didn't love Gretchen; I'm sure she did. But it seemed that she treated her more like a possession than a daughter. There was a cold distance to their interaction, and Mrs. Tanner was constantly watching her like a hawk, criticizing things she did, and ordering her around.

"All I'm saying, Kat," I heard Gretchen start up again, "is that you need to be careful with him. He's a player."

I glanced up at her and nodded.

"It's for your own good," she added. "I wouldn't want to see you get hurt. Do you trust me on this?"

"Totally."

I don't have to tell you that I trusted her about as far as I could throw her, but I also knew there might be more than an ounce of truth to what she was saying. But hadn't Will warned me about Gretchen, as well? Were they both lying or was one the true deceiver? I realized then how isolated I was from people I could rely on—I was now on this road alone.

We didn't talk about Will again for the rest of the night, and after my parents shared a second bottle of wine with the Tanners, everyone air-kissed good-bye, and I drove my family home. When we pulled into the driveway, and before I got out of the car, my mother turned to me gave me a kiss on the cheek.

"Thank you," she said.

"For what?"

"You just made my dream come true."

CHAPTER

22

SO, YEAH, Mom was on cloud nine.

Much as I have should've been right there with her, however, I had a nagging, nervous feeling which I couldn't quite shake. It was about the party. By the time I had checked my e-mail that night, Gretchen had already sent a "save-the-date" Evite to—yes, it's true—the *entire* senior class announcing our party. Now I was locked in and there was no backing out. I should've been thrilled about throwing a blowout with Gretchen—and part of me was—but it just seemed wildly uncharacteristic. And therefore suspicious. Gretchen Tanner was never one to share the limelight. So why now?

I also worried how Dev would react when she heard this latest piece of news. I was sick with the feeling that she would only see this as further evidence, however unfounded, that I'd turned away from her and toward Gretchen. But a way out was nowhere in sight.

Troubled, and knowing that my mother was still up, I wandered downstairs, hoping that maybe if I laid some of my cards on the table, perhaps she could help see me through this. I've always been a little cagey about sharing things with my mother, but what can I say? Sometimes you need your mom. When I reached the foot of the steps, I discovered that she was on the phone with my sister.

"A huge success, Mel. Huge!" I heard my mother say in the family room.

I lingered in the hall.

"Uh-huh . . . uh-huh. . . . and it's all thanks to Katie. The Tanners love her . . . What? I told you, she's totally changed. It's unbelievable!"

I closed my eyes and waited a few more moments.

"You wouldn't even recognize her, Mel. She's totally taken off. It's like . . . Cinderella."

Outside, a gentle breeze blew, rustling the leaves in the trees and rattling our screen door. While my mother continued to sing my praises to my sister, I silently backed away and climbed the steps back to my room.

In the middle of the night, I awoke to the sound of my cell buzzing with a text. Was it Dev? Gretchen? Callie? Groggily, I flipped it open.

WILL: Are u ^

Well, I was now.

KAT: Y—Y R U?

WILL: Need 2 talk

KAT: go ;-)

WILL: In person

I sat straight up. Will wanted to get together . . . now? Why? What was so important that it had to be said in person at three in the morning? I'm not going to lie and say I'd never snuck out before. My junior year Dev and I got caught climbing out my window on our way to see a Blind Bastard concert in New York City. My parents grounded me for a month and told me that if I ever did it again, they would ground me for three months. Even with the success of the dinner with the Tanners, I still couldn't risk it.

KAT: Can't—Rents r crazy

WILL: K. I'll come to u

That shifted my brain into overdrive. The following disjointed thoughts all popped into my head at the same time:

1. *I'm not wearing a bra.*
2. *Are orange pajamas sexy?*
3. *Should I call Callie?*
4. *Pinch yourself and see if you wake up.*

I sprang from bed and ran into my bathroom. It took me a minute to adjust to the light, but I realized soon enough that I looked like a complete and utter disaster. I took a deep breath and put my head under the faucet and drenched my hair straight, and then combed it into a ponytail. I wanted to look a little bit sexy, so I ditched the pj's and changed into a tank top and some boxer shorts. Sitting by my window, I turned on my small bedside lamp and waited. And waited some more.

Ten minutes.

Then fifteen minutes.

Twenty minutes.

When the clock read four a.m., I dozed off, but some time later I heard the sound of a car coming down my street. Craning my neck, I watched as it went by my house, and I thought it must have been somebody else, but then it turned around and slowly came back down the street. The driver shut off the engine maybe fifty feet before reaching my yard and glided up, like a cat on the hunt.

A figure popped out of the car, and sure enough, it was Will. He was wearing frayed khakis, flip-flops, and a white T-shirt.

"Hey," I whispered from my window.

He waved for me to come down.

I put out my index finger and mouthed, "One minute." He nodded and sat down on the porch steps. Thankfully, Remington was about the furthest thing there was from a watchdog, and my parents' room was in the back of the house on the second floor, so I figured we'd be okay. When I pulled the front door open, it creaked—in retrospect, probably no louder than usual, but on that night, in that moment, it sounded like a sonic boom. My heart started racing and my hands shook, but somehow I managed to silently close the door behind me

I stepped outside, and the night air cooled my feet and slid up my uncovered legs. I shivered a little as I walked down the steps to where he was sitting.

"Hi," I said. "We have to whisper. My parents would kill me."

"I know," he said. "I'm sorry, but I really wanted to see you."

Every beat of my heart reverberated throughout my body. Every nerve tingled, from my feet to my hair follicles. I think my brain stopped working, and the words that came out of my mouth were formed by some unknown force that keeps a girl's thoughts in order when the rest of her is falling apart.

"Hey," he said, with a tiny smile. "I'm glad I'm here."

"At my house?"

Apparently this "unknown" force couldn't stop me from being retarded.

He moved closer and put his arm around me. He was warm.

"Thanks," I said. "Why are you up?"

He looked at the stars and didn't say anything for a few moments. His eyes were tired, dark half-moons sagging below them, and while I couldn't say for sure, it seemed like something was weighing on him. Like he was holding a secret he no longer wished to carry.

"I wanted to see you, because I have something I need to tell you. It's important," he said.

"What is it?"

He nodded, and then became silent again.

"I don't believe in promises," he started. I was waiting for the "but" that followed that statement, but again he fell silent. In his eyes I could see a struggle going on. Gretchen's warning slithered through my mind, but I pushed it away.

He took my hands in his, and my heart fluttered.

"I hate the Proud Crowd," he said. "I hate everything about them. Gretchen and her crew. The Black & White Ball. It's all so stupid."

These were not the romantic words I expected.

"But they're your friends, Will. Why are you telling me this?"

He sighed.

"What I'm trying to say is that I like you. A lot. You're so different from them. Whatever you do—don't become one of them."

I wasn't sure how to reply.

"Listen, I have to tell you something more, something that's hard." His voice was trembling a bit.

"What?"

He brought his hands to his head and pulled his hair. For a beat, it seemed like he was going to say something dramatic, but suddenly he smiled.

"Do you want to go to the Black & White Ball with me?"

Has your mind ever short-circuited? I mean, has something a boy said to you ever caused you to momentarily go schizo?

"I'd love to." I grinned. "But aren't we all sitting with Gretchen?"

"Sure. But that doesn't mean that we can't go together. As a couple."

"Are you serious?" I said with a smile. "If you think Gretchen will be okay with it."

He gritted his teeth, and I could see the muscles tense in his jaw, but a beat later he smiled. "Don't worry about her," he said. "I'll take care of it."

In those next moments he gazed into my eyes more deeply than any boy ever had. I felt as though he was stealing my soul. There were no words for what I was feeling, and I knew that was exactly what he was feeling, too. Our hearts were alive together.

Then he leaned in, wrapped his hand around the base of my neck, and kissed me softly on the side of my neck . . . then my ear . . . then my lips . . . then my throat . . . and then he scooped me up and carried me to the hammock just off the porch in the dark. We dropped down into the netting. His lips were soft and his hands were a little rough, but that made me feel oddly safe. I won't lie to you, we got heavy quickly, but being near the porch, and it being my parents' house, and them being but thirty feet away, we kept it under control, for the most part. My heart was pounding and I could feel the blood rushing to my head, to the point where I felt dizzy.

"Let's stop," he said.

"Don't go yet."

"I don't want to, but the sun is coming up, and my mom gets up early."

I looked and, indeed, the first rays of the sun were shining through the tree line.

"Okay."

Suddenly I felt a little weird, like I wanted some confirmation that this night had happened. That he had actually said all those things to me. That we were, I hate to say this, a *couple*.

"No words," he said, putting his finger to my lips and kissing me on the forehead. "No words."

He pulled me up off the hammock and we walked toward the side yard, stopping at the corner of my house. He looked into my eyes for a few moments and held me. His right hand caressed my cheek, and then he turned and walked to the Spitfire. He got in and nodded for me to go inside before he fired it up. And I did, walking backward up the porch stairs, watching him the entire way. After I closed the door, I tiptoed up the stairs to my bedroom window and watched him drive west toward the disappearing moon.

I'd done it. I was going to the Black & White Ball with Will. I'd gotten exactly what I'd wanted. I had an urge to call Dev right then and tell her everything that had happened and find a way to patch things up with her; but somehow it didn't feel right. Will? The Black & White? It was all real now, but it felt nothing like I imagined it would. It felt empty and thrilling all at once, and it left me feeling jittery and unsure and alive in a way I'd never felt before.

BOOK FIVE

. . . .

THE CRASH

CHAPTER

23

THE THING ABOUT the Market was that even when you thought you should get out, there was something sucking you right back in. In the business world they call it Golden Handcuffs. You may know that you should quit, but the high life becomes so addictive that you're essentially imprisoned by it—and so it was with me. I became more and more obsessed with making it to the top of the Market. Soon after making Blue Chip status, the bloom was off the rose and Nine (my ranking as of 5/15) seemed incredibly low. It was like I'd hit a glass ceiling. Carrie Bell was still above me? Nina Licht? C'mon! Now that I'd had a taste of being ranked high, I wanted to be at the very top. Number One. Remarkably, the portfolio Dev, Callie, and I opened was right near the top in the rankings—our only real competitor was the same one Callie had pointed out to me weeks before: TKWP. It had moved in lock step with ours.

But after four weeks of ups and downs on the Market, and more than a handful of sleepless nights, I was worn out. On paper I may have been living the dream, but inside, I could feel something twisting—torquing my very being. Was this what it felt like to finally come out of one's cocoon, or was my soul getting perverted into something I never wanted it to be?

On the Wednesday before the Black & White, I was due to have my going-away dinner with Mrs. Sawyer. While I'd been feeling a bit reclusive most of the day, I decided I was going to put on a happy face and deal, because this was one date on which I could not bail.

We met at Louise Morel's, a little French bistro on North Adams Street. Before coming back home to Millbank to open the BookStop, Mrs. Sawyer lived in Paris for four years. She loved all things Parisian. I think outside of Howie and the store, her romance with the City of Light was the most meaningful relationship of her life. She was already sipping on a glass of wine when I arrived, and I ordered a wineglass of cranberry juice and pretended we were on the Left Bank. We easily fell into conversation, mostly memories of my time at the BookStop, Howie stories (a topic we often bonded over), and my plans for college. It wasn't until dessert was served that she surprised me with a question I expected more from my mother than from my boss.

"Are you happy, Kate?" she asked. "With the new you?"

I hadn't been aware of it, but Mrs. Sawyer had obviously been keeping tabs on me.

"What do you mean?" I asked. "I really haven't changed. It's just some new clothes."

"That's true," she said. "How's your mom's quest to get into the club?"

"Oh, ridiculous as ever," I quipped. "On Monday, we all had to get dressed up and have dinner with the Tanners."

"Oh, yes. He's nice. Mr. Tanner, that is."

"He is," I said. "But she sort of creeped me out."

"Why do you think your mom wants to get in the club so badly?" she asked.

It was a good question, one to which I'd never found a satisfactory answer.

"Maybe because she grew up in this town. Maybe she's proving something to herself?"

Mrs. Sawyer took a sip of wine and then she looked over toward the old high school building across the street that was now used as a YMCA. "I went to school when it was over there," she said, pointing with her free hand. "The Black & White Ball was the thing then, suppose it still is."

"Did you go?"

"Me, no. We were too poor. And they didn't let

blacks go to the dance—or in the club."

She took another sip. I felt foolish for not knowing that and even more foolish for my mother for trying to get into the club.

"I'm sorry," I said, not knowing what else to say. "I didn't know."

"Why would you?" she said. "They let everyone in now . . . if you have the money. They've come a long way—it doesn't matter if you're black or white or yellow or stupid or smart or one-eyed or two," she said, and then whispered, "As long as you're the right *kind* of person." And then she started laughing. I couldn't help but laugh with her—I'd never seen her so amused.

"Right." I smiled. "I imagine all the women are just like Gretchen and Mrs. Tanner."

"I imagine so," said Mrs. Sawyer. "Is that who you're trying to be?"

That's when the laughing stopped. At least, my laughing. Somehow Mrs. Sawyer had tricked me into her little trap.

"No," I said. "I don't want to be her."

I looked down at what remained of my dessert and suddenly felt like I couldn't eat another bite. A few moments passed before either of us said anything.

"I didn't mean to upset you, Kate," she said.

"I know, but it wasn't like that. Dev and I just wanted to beat the Market."

"The Market?"

"Some people—boys, I guess—in school started a Web site that rated all the girls. It's like a stock market, but girls are traded. It's disgusting, really."

"It sounds it," she said. "And you were low, I assume, and wanted to be higher, is that right?"

"Yes," I said. "It sounds worse having you say it."

Then she surprised me. "I think you did the right thing," she concluded, not meeting my eye. "Sometimes you have to work within the system before you can change it." Then she took her last swallow of wine. "And you beat it, I suppose?"

"Yeah, pretty much," I said, kind of giddy now that I had her approval.

"Mm-hmm," she said. "That's good. So tell me now, what is it you are going to do to change it?"

I didn't have an answer. I had been so busy climbing the ladder that by the time I got to the top I had simply forgotten how—and why—I'd gotten here.

"There's no time left—graduation is next week. There's really no time to change anything," I said.

I knew it was lame as soon as it came out of my mouth. More importantly, I knew she wouldn't believe me.

She sort of nodded, and a beat later asked the waiter for another glass of wine. We sat there for another half hour, chatting about unimportant things, but what she'd said echoed in my head and in my heart: what was I going to do to change things? Sadly, I had no answer. I didn't even know if I had the desire.

I drove south across River Road and headed in a direction that was the opposite of my home. In the past few days I'd taken up a little habit that I hadn't told anyone about. I liked to drive by Will's house, hoping to catch a glimpse of him in his bedroom window. It was sort of childish, I know, but this is what a huge crush will do to you. It was a dark, moonless night, so I had my high beams on as I drove down South Adams and took a right onto West Main. He lived on a little street called Soos Circle, and as I turned, I cut off my beams and coasted toward the end of the cul de sac. His light was on, and I could see his silhouette behind a shade. He was sitting with his feet up and if I had to guess, he was typing on his computer. There in our separate worlds, divided maybe by fifty feet, I wondered if that person, the boy, had been worth everything I'd done.

When I arrived home, my father was sitting on the front porch, nursing a bottle of Stella Artois—his favorite beer. In that form of silent communication you have with a parent, I didn't even wave as I approached. I just walked up the steps and sat down next to him on the retro 1950s glider that had stood underneath the picture window off the dining room for as long as I can remember. It was rusting on the edges, squeaked a bit when you moved, but there was a comfortable familiarity in it.

We sat there quietly for a few moments, and without looking over, he offered me a sip of his beer. Dad had offered me "swigs"—as he put it—of his beer since I was a little girl. It used to drive Mom crazy, and she told him to stop, but he always argued that if he let me have a little alcohol now, it wouldn't be such a forbidden fruit later. He'd been right.

Gently, I took the bottle from his hand and took a sip. A beat later, I handed it back to him and he nodded.

"I don't want to join Mom's club," he said.

"Did you tell her that?"

"No," he answered. "I don't really have the heart."

"It means a lot to her."

"Sadly, it means a lot to a fair amount of people," he remarked. "I never understood it."

"I do," I said. "I do."

He looked over at me quizzically, waiting for more, but I didn't answer his gaze. It was too much for me to explain, and I wasn't sure he'd get it, even if I did.

"Well, I prefer this club right here," he said, and he put his arm around me.

Across the street, a television snapped on in an otherwise black room, and I reached over for another sip.

CHAPTER

24

CLAD IN OUR BIKINIS, Gretchen and I were lying out on
the balcony off her bedroom soaking in the Thursday afternoon sun. Ostensibly I was there to work on planning the
graduation party with her, but after an hour our will had
waned and we decided that a little tan would be a good idea.
Memorial Day was right around the corner, after all, and as
Gretchen was quick to point out, nothing looked worse than
pasty skin against a white dress.

"It's *so* white trash," she'd declared.

Half an hour later, Art (the Tanners' cook) brought us
some fresh beef teriyaki lettuce wraps, along with a few bottles of San Pellegrino and dessert. Supposedly, the masseuse
was coming over at seven p.m. so the Tanners could get their
massages, and Mrs. Tanner invited me to get one as well.

Yeah, I could get used to this.

"So I'm thinking the invitations should be blue and gold—sort of like our graduation gowns," Gretchen mused, eyes closed against the sun. "We'll get them rush printed at Kate's Paperie. We only have ten days."

"I thought you said that invitations are only for sixth graders."

Wasn't that the critique she'd leveled me with that time I came to her party?

"Hel-lo," she replied as she grabbed the Evian mister and sprayed herself. "For a get-together, yes. But this is a *real* party. You have to take it seriously."

"Got it," I answered and sat up.

Art had also baked us some fudge brownies that—though melting in the sun—were tempting me just a few feet away. Gretchen, however, hadn't touched them, so I figured I shouldn't either. I snagged a piece of celery and swirled it around in the ranch dressing before munching down. I may have come a long way, but sitting side by side with Gretchen in a bikini was a pretty sobering reality check. My midsection was a little soft; hers had been ab-blasted and was chiseled.

"Besides, you have to tell people what to wear," she continued. "We don't want people showing up like slobs. We'll call for 'casual chic.'"

"Good idea."

"And we have to get the DJ who played at Elisa's sweet sixteen. He was the best."

A cool breeze blew in from the west, and the tops of the trees on the edge of the Tanners' property swayed, leaves fluttering up and down. Feeling a chill, I pulled up my towel from the lounge and wrapped it around my shoulders.

"Thanks for doing all this," I said.

"Please, it's nothing," she answered, rolling onto her side. "What we really have to do is find you a cool dress. You have a reputation to live up to now."

"How do you mean?"

Gretchen stared at me for a beat and then smiled. Pushing herself to her feet, she disappeared into her room before returning shortly with a small velvet box. She handed it to me.

"What is it?"

"Just open it."

When I did, I felt my eyes go wide. Inside the box was a silver "P"—the same one that all the girls in the Proud Crowd wore. I couldn't quite believe what I was seeing.

"Is this . . . for me?"

Gretchen nodded. "You're one of us now."

I slipped the "P" from the box and guided its silver chain around my neck. The metal was cold against my skin, and I was at a complete and total loss for words. I was now officially one of the Proud Crowd.

"Wow," I mumbled in shock.

"You're a Blue Chipper, babe."

The mention of the Market smashed through my revelry, and try as I did to blink away my thoughts, the moment was tainted.

"Do you ever worry about it?" I finally asked, looking up at her. "Does it bother you?"

"What? The Market? I don't really think about it."

"C'mon," I challenged back. "I know you're Number One and all that, but it has to have an effect on you. You're telling me you never look at it?"

She pursed her lips and considered what I was saying.

"Sure, I look at it," she confessed. "But things like that aren't, like, isolated. You think it's any different from *People* magazine or Page Six or any of those blogs tracking stars? It's all the same."

"We're not celebrities, Gretchen."

"We are in this pond, Kate. No matter who you are, somebody's judging you."

"Like your mom?"

I actually hadn't even considered the full import of what I was saying before I spoke, and immediately I wanted to kick myself—assuming, of course, that I could've gotten my foot out of my mouth.

But just when I was expecting Gretchen to rip me in two, her expression cracked ever so slightly and I caught a glimpse, however fleeting, of the little girl beneath the It Girl. She looked away and wrinkled her nose. I wondered then, that cocooned as she was by her ass-kissing friends, if anyone ever had the nerve to point things out to her as they really were.

As if wary of revealing too much, she pulled the rubber band from her ponytail and flipped her hair behind her shoulders. "Just get used to it, Kate," she breathed. "The sooner you do, the better off you'll be."

I wanted to contradict her, to tell her that I knew, in fact, that it didn't have to be that way. Don't ask me why I was suddenly on a mission to save Gretchen Tanner; I was probably the one who needed saving, after all. But before I could say anything, Gretchen's cell rang. In an instant, her all-knowing smile returned, and she flipped open her phone.

"Hey, Pip!" she gushed. Then she mouthed to me: "It's Will."

I felt my jaw clench. Was "Pip" her pet name for him?

"You don't mind if I take this, right?" she asked as she covered the mouthpiece.

I shook my head, and Gretchen retreated into her bedroom, leaving me alone on the balcony. It's no news flash to report that it made me crazy that Will was calling Gretchen, but my rational side, which I'll fully acknowledge was waging an uphill battle, kept reminding me there was nothing strange about Will talking with Gretchen. They were good friends, had been long before I ever entered the picture, so what was my issue?

Well, I'll tell you exactly what my issue was.

It was Gretchen laughing a little too loudly at everything Will said. It was Gretchen calling him "hon" every third sentence. It was Gretchen telling him that she'd "swing by his house later" when she was "alone" so they could "chitty-chat." I was pretty sure she was playing it all up for my sake—I was no dummy—but regardless, jealousy constricted my body, and I grabbed my jeans from the balustrade and slipped them over my bathing suit. If I was about to wage war, I'd also better be ready to flee.

A few seconds later, Gretchen said 'bye to Will and although fuming, I forced a smile. "How's Will?"

"Just Will being Will," she answered, and tossed her cell on the lounge. "He's so sweet, though."

"It's true." I nodded as I started lining up my shot.

I knew I was playing with fire, but I just couldn't help myself.

After a carefully calculated few seconds, I inhaled sharply and allowed my mouth to fall open ever so slightly. "Omigod, I totally meant to tell you. The strangest thing happened the other night."

"What?"

"Will came over to my house—really late. And he asked me if I'd go to the Black & White with him."

"What are you talking about? You're both sitting at my table."

"I know, but he said he wanted to go together. You know"—I paused here for effect—"he wants to go as a couple."

Now, Einstein tells us that the passage of time is relative to the observer, and I swear in that moment, it was as if time stood still. Gretchen was frozen, immobile, not flinching, not even blinking as she processed the news. I don't know how long we both remained like that, eye to eye, but it felt like an eternity.

"Good for you," she cooed. "That's *sooooo* great."

"I know you warned me about him," I continued. "But I figured it's just one night. What's the harm, right?"

Gretchen picked up a brownie and took a bite. "Totally. But you're still going to hang with me and the girls, right?"

"Duh." I smiled and put my hand on her shoulder. "You're my girl."

"Remember it," she answered, and looked out at her pool thoughtfully. "I'm just going to get changed and then we need to finish planning things. Okay?"

I nodded, and Gretchen grabbed her towel and left. Standing alone on the balcony, I suddenly worried if it had been a mistake to tell Gretchen. Well, I would've had to at some point anyway. She was going to see me there with Will, so it wasn't going to stay a secret forever.

No, I was right to have done what I did. Gretchen and I may have been becoming "friends," but she needed to know who she was dealing with. Slipping my T-shirt back on, I took one last look at the now-setting sun, and walked back into Gretchen's darkening room.

KCW LLC.

MARKET RANKING: 4
TODAY'S CHANGE: ↑1

SHARE PRICE: $35.06
   CHANGE: ↑4.06 (+12%)
L/B RATIO: 10.2
3-MONTH RANGE: $1.23–$35.18
STATUS: BLUE CHIP

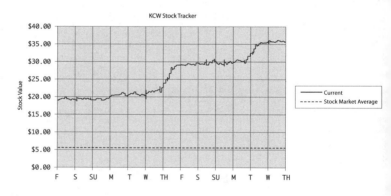

ANALYST RECOMMENDATION: The only question that needs answering is how long it will be until this performer is #1.

DEFINITE BUY

CHAPTER

25

THE NEXT THIRTY-SIX hours passed in a blur of preparations for the Black & White. Having my hair blown out at Images, a manicure from Nailtiques downtown, even a facial in New York at this spa, Cornelia—I was on a whirlwind beauty tour, this time courtesy of my mother. Mom was so fired up about the Black & White that she even wrote me a note so I could get out of school early on Friday, and we drove into the city (a *second* time) to check out a dress by Michael Kors. Apparently, the one we'd already picked out from Nordstrom wasn't good enough. The latest dress was a stunning white number, which is the color all the women wore, that Mom discovered online. Tiered with a lace border, it did a lot for my body, but when I looked at the price tag, I thought I was going to have a heart attack. True to character, Mom was adamant that her daughter look her best for what basically amounted to my coming out, and with a confident nod, she calmly reached into her purse and plunked down her credit card next to the cash register.

When I wasn't transforming myself into a mannequin for the Black & White, I was planning the big graduation party with Gretchen. To be honest, she was doing most of the planning—I performed more of a "yes, ma'am" role— but kids at school kept coming up to me asking if they should bring anything and whether Gretchen and I were going to let juniors or kids from any other schools come. Word had traveled far and wide. While I enjoyed all the attention, it also wasn't lost on me that up until four weeks ago, I'd had barely a passing acquaintance with ninety-nine percent of these people. My true friends, or at least those who had been so before the Market began, had said nothing about the party. I'd sent e-mails and texts, and left voice mails for Dev, but she'd never replied. I prayed that when the three of us sat down on Saturday, we'd be able to set everything right. If I could just look her in the eye, and she could see how sincere my intentions were and also how honest my apology was, she'd forgive me.

Through it all, there was the Market. I was constantly checking it, poring over the analyst's recommendations, obsessed with my ranking, and even when I had no access to a computer, Gretchen would gleefully call me with updates.

Hour by hour my stock value kept climbing, ultimately passing Carrie and Elisa. By now, these incremental steps barely registered, determined as I was to make it to the top, and when I logged on to the Market Friday night and discovered I was now ranked Number Two—with only Gretchen above me—I didn't even bat an eye.

I awoke Saturday to a spring morning. My room was filled with crisp cool air, and bright light filtered in through my shades.

"I'm going to the Black & White with Will," I heard myself say. It was a veritable fairy tale end to my high school career.

I was still in a sleepy daze, but I soon recognized my mother's voice calling my name.

"Kate! Callie's on the phone!"

I looked over at my clock, and in an instant, I realized that I'd overslept. I was supposed to meet Dev and Callie at the Cozy Corner at 9:00 a.m. for the dreaded powwow. It was already 9:30 a.m.

Sh—!

"Tell her I already left," I shouted. I threw on some old sweats, splashed some water on my face, and grabbed my keys and ran downstairs. I could see my mom was still talking to her on the phone, so I tiptoed by and zipped out to my car.

By the time I got into town and had parked, it was nearly ten. As I hurried down the sidewalk, through the plate glass window I could see Dev and Callie holding court in our corner booth, and neither looked too happy.

"Hey," I said as I slipped into the booth. "Sorry I got a late start. My alarm never went off."

That much was true.

"Right," Callie said. "We ordered you coffee and toast."

"Thanks."

Callie took a sip of her coffee, but her eyes never left me. Dev, on the other hand, wouldn't even look my way, and her stare remained glued to her hands that were folded in her lap.

"So," I opened, as I shredded the corner of my napkin.

Callie glanced over at Dev for support. "We're concerned about you."

"Concerned?" I frowned. "Why?"

Dev sighed and looked up. "I think this experiment—this quest to beat the Market—has gone to your head."

I took a deep breath to collect myself.

"Look, I understand that you felt blindsided by what happened with Gretchen. And I apologize for that. I really hope you can forgive me. It wasn't cool."

"That's one way of putting it."

"Dev," I said as I touched her hand. "I'm really *sorry*. Honestly."

If I was hoping that she'd smile, and we'd have a make-up laugh about it, nothing of the sort was forthcoming.

"I hate to say it, but you've gotten so wrapped up in the Market, that you can't see what's going on," Dev finally said. "You're in too deep."

The tone of this conversation was less like reconciliation, and more like confrontation. I felt myself mentally backpedaling in confusion. My toast and coffee arrived, and there was a welcome pause in the conversation.

"I got in too deep?" I asked as delicately as I could. "Dev, whose idea was the experiment in the first place? Who was the person who thought we could beat the system? Who pulled me out of class and pretended my grandfather died? Who e-mailed my rising and falling numbers almost hourly until I became so neurotic about it I couldn't sleep at night?"

"Is that true?" Callie asked, looking at Dev in disgust. "I knew this thing would make you two crazy."

"Okay, I got a little excited," Dev said, waving me off. "But we're getting off topic here."

"Fine," I snorted as I started to become frustrated. "What is the topic exactly?"

Dev put her face in her hands, and Callie looked out at the street nervously.

"It's about the TKWP portfolio," Dev began.

So here it was. Dev was finally going to admit that she

was the one behind it from the very beginning. Well, it was better that we get everything out on the table.

"TKWP, you see . . ." Dev hesitated. "It think it's Gretchen and Will."

I laughed.

"Kate, really. Dev explained it to me last night. It sounds legit," Callie seconded.

Dev leaned forward. "They've been using you the whole time."

I read in AP Bio once that when the human body switches into fight-or-flight mode, there's a literal narrowing of the field of vision, almost as if you're looking through a tube. Well, that's how I felt right then, and I was totally targeted in on Dev; and I was in fight mode.

"You've got to be kidding—"

"Kate, it's true!" Dev said.

"No, it isn't!" I fired back as rage, like a snake, spiraled up inside me. All my goodwill disintegrated in an instant. "You're just jealous that I'm going to the Black & White with Will. You wish you were me. Why can't you be happy instead of trying to tear me down?"

"Because it's all a front!" Dev shouted.

"Will's in love with me!"

Dev grew quiet for a moment and looked down at the table. "No, he isn't."

There aren't words to express the fury I was feeling. Just

because I'd moved past Dev, here she was trying to tear me down. Yes, that's exactly what it was.

"Let's all try to be cool here," Callie calmed us. "Just think, Kate. Their portfolio has gone up equally with ours."

"Do you think that it's an accident that you ended up at Gretchen's party?" Dev asked, still hot. "That Will asked you out? That Gretchen's suddenly your new best friend? They've been playing you."

"No, it's no accident. It's because people finally saw the real me."

"What they saw was the perfect mark, or in this case, the perfect stock," Dev fired back. "You were beautiful but untapped, hidden from the world of Millbank High. At Seventy-one your value was well below what it should've been. That's totally true. But you were just a racehorse to them—a long shot that had good odds of coming in."

Doubt crept into my mind for the first time, but I pushed it away.

"Let me tell you what I think," I spat. "Maybe *you're* TKWP."

Dev looked like somebody had hit her with a baseball bat. Next to her, Callie put her face in her hands.

"Why else would you have been so obsessed with my popularity?" I continued. "Goading me on like a lunatic. Maybe—"

"Are you serious?!" Dev said. "You've gone off your friggin' rocker! TKWP—think about it! The Kate Winthrop Project!"

Suddenly, it all seemed too real. I fell silent.

Across from me, Dev's face went blotchy, and tears began to form in the corners of her big brown eyes. "You're an idiot, Kate," she whispered as her lips quivered. "Do you know what it's like to be me? Five feet two with a squat ass and a plain face? Do you?"

I couldn't say anything. My mouth was frozen and my head spun wildly with emotion—both enraged at what she'd said and saddened to see her so upset.

"You were always one step from beautiful, from having it all," Dev explained. "I'm miles away, and for a couple of weeks I wanted to be you, to be climbing the ladder with you, I suppose. And this is what I get."

Dev burst into tears before Callie put an arm around her and gave her a hug as she sobbed.

Guilt. Well, that's a word that doesn't quite describe the hollow feeling that was in my gut. If I could take back the last fifteen minutes, I would have given everything up, even Will and the Black & White. Everything.

Confusion swept through me, and suddenly the only thing I did know for certain was that I had to get out of there. Without another word, I got up, threw five dollars on the table, and walked right out of the restaurant. Tears now began to pour from my eyes, and as I got to my car, I couldn't catch my breath.

Could it be?

The Gretchen stuff—well, that much seemed plausible. I'd had my suspicions about her right from the beginning. And hadn't she done her paper on Michael Milken? But Will? Had everything we'd done together—every word he'd whispered in my ear, every caress of his hand—been a total lie? It was unfathomable, but if true, the single cruelest thing ever done to me. I sat there for a half hour, unable to drive, unable to move, feeling nothing but nausea rising in my throat. In nine hours I was supposed to be on the arm of Will, waltzing into the Black & White with my new friends. Tonight had had the promise of being everything I had ever imagined high school could be, and now it was becoming everything that high school actually was: heart-breaking and cruel.

I looked up from my car window and saw Callie, like the bighearted mother she was, walking Dev out of the Cozy Corner. Her arm was around Dev, who was still sobbing, and she was saying something to her. As they disappeared around the corner, I knew I was truly alone, and I understood then that sitting on top of the world just meant you were all by yourself.

CHAPTER

26

IT WAS SEVEN O'CLOCK and I was sitting on my bed, staring at my white dress hanging beneath its clear plastic sheeting. Mom had knocked no less than five times in the last hour to see if I needed any help, but with my door locked I was hidden from everyone, desperately trying to figure out what to do.

The intervening hours since the big scene with the girls had done nothing to soothe my aching heart and tortured mind. With dark suspicion planted, right when I should've been in some state of breathless anticipation for the big night ahead, I was instead looking backward, replaying everything that had happened to me, starting at Gretchen's party. And much as I didn't want to believe any of it, when I really broke down every step that Gretchen took, it began to become more and more clear that reasonable doubt was not in her favor. The episodes flashed through my mind like a prosecutor's slide show before a jury: the invitation to her party where she first mentioned the Market, the late-night IM taunting me to look at the Web site, the number scrawled on my locker, inviting me to hang with her and the girls, planning the big end-of-the-year party together—Gretchen had crafted it all meticulously. Worse, I'd allowed myself to be hypnotized into believing it was all real.

The question that still loomed was why? For money? Gretchen was totally loaded; she didn't need to win the game. For pride? To show that she was the ultimate social manipulator?

But the biggest question I couldn't answer for myself—and undoubtedly the most important—was Will himself. Let's say he was involved, let's say he'd been in on it with Gretchen from the beginning. I guess I could make sense of all the moves he'd made except one: the night he came to my house and asked me to the Black & White. If he weren't truly in love with me, why would he bother? I clung to that night as evidence of his love for me. Otherwise I was lost.

I walked toward my closet, tossed the white dress aside, and took out a black one that Callie had loaned me ages ago. Silk with spaghetti straps and a plunging back that dropped just to the tip of my tailbone, it was just the dress for the evening. If I were going, then I was going to make a statement, and not wearing white was the only way I could think of reclaiming a little bit of myself. I didn't know how I was going to do it exactly, but I had to find out for sure if Will was really behind the portfolio. Obviously, I couldn't come straight out and ask him, because if he wasn't involved, I'd look like the fool. But if he was, I wanted to look him in the eyes when he confessed.

Come 7:30 p.m. when the doorbell rang announcing Will's arrival, I was dressed head to toe in black. The two exceptions were my mother's beautiful string of pearls and the little silver "P" Gretchen had given me. I knew my mom would go crazy when she saw me not wearing white, but I was banking on the fact that she wouldn't say anything once Will was there.

I opened the door to my room and slowly walked across the hallway and stopped at the stairwell. I could hear my mother talking to Will in that way mothers talk to their daughter's boyfriends—somewhere between flirty and complimentary—and I walked down the stairs as quietly as I could. I didn't capture their attention until I hit the landing, when Will's eyes lit up and gave me that up-and-down that all boys give girls. Shock at the black was quickly followed by an approving grin, and it was clear that he liked what he was seeing.

But when my mother turned and gave me the up-and-down, unlike Will, she was less than pleased.

"Kate," she snapped. "In the kitchen for a second, please."

I looked at Will and then back at my mom. My dad was standing behind her, totally oblivious to what was going on.

"Mom, we're late."

She shot me an icy stare, and I felt the hairs on the back of my neck tingle.

"It'll just take a second."

I really couldn't get around it, so I relented and followed her to the kitchen, but I wasn't going to fold, either. My entire identity had been destroyed earlier in the day, and this mild protest was all I had left of my self-esteem. I wasn't going to let my mother take it away.

"You can't wear that," she fumed once we were out of earshot. "You have to wear white."

"Says who? That dumb club?"

I thought her eyeballs were going to pop out of her head.

"You're going to go change—right now! We spent a lot of money on that white dress."

"I know. So now you can return it."

Her fists clenched at her side. "It's the tradition, Kate—what will Gretchen say?"

"I don't care what Gretchen or you or anybody else says!"

"Why do you always have to make things difficult?" my mother shot back.

"Difficult—you mean difficult for you, right?"

"I'm not the one going to the ball."

"No. You're just worried about getting in this stupid club that no one else wants to be part of. Not me. Not Dad. It's all about you and your stupid insecurities!"

"That's enough!" she shouted, and in a flash, her hand flew up and slapped me across the face. She had never hit me before. Tears formed in my eyes, but I willed myself not to give her the satisfaction. Not that she got any. I could see her eyes go from angry to sad in about a millisecond, and she stepped back, not quite comprehending what she had just done.

Without a word, I turned and pushed through the swinging kitchen door and went straight for the foyer. When I reached the front door, I snatched my purse from the table and pushed by Will. Behind me, I heard him offer polite good-byes to my parents before following me like a puppy dog to the car.

When he got in, he looked over at me. "You cool?"

"Let's go."

I sat in silence the entire drive to the dance. Will tried a few questions at first, but when he got no response, not even eye contact, he barreled ahead, the Spitfire growling beneath us.

At a red light, where Forest Avenue crosses Piedmont, he pulled to a stop, and for a few moments there was relative calm. Around us I could hear crickets sawing away in the trees. Turning in his seat, Will reached over and touched my welted cheek with the outside of his hand. I didn't respond—didn't smile, didn't recoil—but inside, the pieces of my heart were shattering a little bit more. I wanted to believe that he loved me or was at least falling in love with me, but every gesture, no matter how tender, was met with the continuing echo of Dev's words: *he's using you.*

The light turned green, and his hand dropped to the gearshift. For a split second there was the gunning of the engine before we lurched forward, my back pressed into the seat.

We pulled in front of the club and were met by an army of valets, who scooped us from our car and set us on the black-and-white carpet. It felt like we were walking into the Academy Awards. Flashes popped, photographers shouted, and guests greeted each other with air kisses as a parade of beauty and wealth glided down the carpet toward the entrance of the club. My black dress raised eyebrows on a few of the old biddies, but I shook it off and held my head high.

Peppered among the crowd—heads constantly rotating, nervously sizing up other people's outfits—were a handful of my mom's friends. Even though they were all members of the club, I couldn't help but notice how they were comparing themselves to other people—the clothing they were wearing, the jewelry that dangled from their wrists and necks. I realized then that my mom and I weren't really that different. We were both chasing popularity, that elusive circle of status that doesn't really exist. It's always one circle away, unattainable. It struck me that there's only a two-letter difference between "exclusive" and "elusive." I shuddered for a moment with guilt, realizing that I had made accusations at Mom that I should have been leveling at myself.

The ballroom, cavernous and barren when Will had given me the tour of the club, now overflowed with guests. Tables of hors d'oeuvres with ice-sculpture centerpieces flanked the dance floor, and tuxedo-clad waiters, balancing silver trays of champagne, wine, and daiquiris, skated through the crowd. On a stage, a twenty-piece band cranked out an odd assortment of songs, and while no one had ventured as yet to dance, guests young and old swayed to the rhythm among the safety of tables. The whole scene had an otherworldly quality to it, like we'd just entered a time warp, and I thought to myself that this was no different than a ball at Versailles in the eighteenth century, a reception at the Taj Mahal in the seventeenth, or no doubt what was happening tonight in some club in Kansas or Oregon. The history of man was one long repetition.

As Will and I wove our way through the revelers, I spotted Jack on the other side of the room. Impeccably dressed, he leaned against the wall, chatting amiably with a bevy of girls. For a split second, our eyes met—I'm sure of it—but he showed no trace of a reaction and continued on with his conversation.

At last, Will and I arrived at our table. Gretchen, her girls, and the elite of the Proud Crowd were already there, laughing and enjoying the scene. My black dress caught the eye of every girl, but I nodded to everyone and silently took my seat.

It was Gretchen who finally acknowledged what they were all thinking.

"Didn't Will tell you, Kat?" Gretchen grinned. "The ladies wear white."

I didn't respond. I gave her a calm stare, one I suspect an assassin develops over a career. It was pure indifference and I could tell it bothered her.

"What's wrong?" she said. "I was just teasing you."

My face remained flat. I looked into her eyes for a moment, but with a deadness that disarmed her even more.

I turned to Will.

"I feel like dancing," I announced. He looked around, a little surprised. The dance floor was entirely empty, and the band was playing a very slow instrumental, but I stood up and grabbed his hand, leading him to the dance floor. As we crossed the parquet, I could feel eyes on my bare back, my blond hair coiffed to perfection; but my pulse didn't flicker. I felt cold as ice.

I pulled Will close to me, and we rocked back and forth together. As we spun there on the wood floor, the chandelier glowing softly above, I noticed that most of the room was watching us. I suppose on the surface we looked like the perfect couple. Men nodded. Women smiled. The little girl inside me who'd always dreamed of a fantastical night like this wanted everything to be right, everything to be a storybook ending; but my now-tired soul told me that it was going to be something far different. Something within me kept whispering the truth, and by now it seemed unavoidable. I suppose Will must've known that something was up, because for all his cool, I could feel his hands trembling and his heart pounding. I pulled him to me as tight as two humans could be on a dance floor.

As we turned, I looked up and caught Gretchen's eyes following us. She was as furious as I've ever seen her. It was then that I started nibbling on his ear, in a cute sexy way, and Gretchen averted her gaze, the veins in her forehead showing.

I whispered in his ear, "Gretchen's watching us."

His back tightened.

"Ignore her."

"I will, if you can."

He stopped dancing and pulled away from me just enough to look me in the eyes. There was sadness there, and he fumbled over some words before he was able to put together something coherent.

"What are you doing?" he asked.

"Just making sure I'm not upsetting anything between the two of you."

"We're done, Gretchen and I. I've told you that before."

"But you're a team?" I said.

He looked at me funny. And then a glimmer of recognition lit his eyes.

"What do you mean, team?"

"I think you know what I mean, Will."

"No I don't—what'd she say?"

"Nothing, she said nothing. It was you, remember? I was the girl you couldn't see. But you really could see me—I was Number Seventy-one and a perfect mark for the little game you and Gretchen were playing. TKWP—The Kate Winthrop Project—how clever. Did you come up with that name yourself or do you just take credit for it, like Jack's songs?"

His face froze. He tried to speak but nothing came out. His eyes looked all around, but couldn't hold mine.

If there had been a drop of hope that this all might end right, it evaporated.

"You don't understand," he said. "I really fell for you. I think I love you."

My right hand came up like a flash, and it smacked against his face harder than I expected, and the Black & White suddenly became the quiet and stupefied. It was like all the oxygen in the room had been sucked right out. Hands went to mouths, and then mouths went to ears, and the place buzzed.

I turned and walked toward the table to get my purse.

"Kate!" Will called, but I didn't stop.

Gretchen stood up and blocked the walkway between the two tables.

"What the hell are you doing?"

"Drop the bullshit, Gretchen. I know about TKWP."

Unfazed as ever, she smirked and shot a look over at her friends. "This is a good lesson, guys. If something's cheap— there's always a reason."

I looked at her and then at the table of her sycophants. It made me sick to think that I had spent even one night with them. Just then a waiter walked by with a tray of virgin strawberry daiquiris—thick and red and icy. I reached over and grabbed one off the tray.

"Tasty," I observed after taking the tiniest of sips. "Why don't you try some."

And in one fluid motion, I tossed the contents of the entire glass on the front of her pure white dress. All of her friends screamed before she could. Like someone who'd just been shot—by a very big gun, mind you—she stared down at the front of her dress, soaked bloodred, completely slack jawed and speechless.

My hands shaking, I plunked the glass down on the

table, grabbed my clutch, and ran out of the room. Careening down the black-and-white carpet, there were no pictures being taken of me this time, and as I reached the front door of the club, a hand grabbed my arm. I turned with a balled-up fist, thinking it was either Gretchen or one of her friends . . . but it was Will.

"Wait."

Tears were swamping his eyes, and his face was contorted in pain.

"Wait," he repeated.

"For you? I'd rather die."

I tore my arm free and raced out into the pitch-black night.

Ten minutes later, I stumbled along the shoulder of the road, black mascara-laden tears running down my cheeks and my broken heels in my hands. A thin drizzle spitted down from the sky, and every now and then a car would pass, tires shushing on the wet pavement. In between sobs, I cursed Will and Gretchen and the day I met them both, and wondered how I'd ever allowed myself to fall for their deception.

Illuminated by the headlights of a car approaching from behind, my dark shadow stretched out far ahead of me, and I veered to the right, away from the road. As the car neared, however, the sound of the engine quieted, and as it pulled alongside me, it drew to a stop. The driver beeped his horn.

Nervously, I glanced over. The windows were tinted and I didn't recognize the car, so instead of trying to figure out who it was—one of Gretchen's girls? some freak?—I picked up my pace. The car glided forward and pulled up beside me again. Against my better judgment, which was telling me to run, my emotions got the better of me, and I turned toward the driver and screamed.

"What do you want?!"

There was no response, but a beat later the window lowered and my fear-cum-anger melted.

It was Jack.

"Get in," he said simply.

Embarrassed, horrified, wrong—none of it mattered anymore, and after glancing down the pitch-black road, I opened the door and dropped into the passenger seat. I closed the door, which shut with a reassuring *clump*, and put my face in my hands. We didn't say anything to each other the whole way back to my house. He drove silently; I continued to cry. When we reached my driveway, I wiped my tears away and found Jack looking at me, concern in his eyes.

"Did you know?" I asked.

"About the Market?" He nodded. "But about them?" He shook his head.

I looked down.

"I'm sorry," he said.

I nodded, and after a barely audible "Thank you," my throat choked with emotion, and I staggered into my house.

BOOK SIX

· · · · · · ·

DIVIDENDS

CHAPTER

27

I DIDN'T GET UP for nearly an entire day. Not the phone ringing, not my mother's vacuuming, not my heart's rending could rouse me. When the sun had come and gone, and the darkness of night returned, I finally staggered out of bed. When I bumped into my desk as I made my way to the bathroom, my computer woke from sleep mode and the Market flashed up on the screen. For a split second, I considered looking at my ranking, just to see how far I'd fallen, but an instant later I yanked the cord from the outlet, and the monitor went black.

First things first (as my mom is fond of saying)—if I wanted to get back on the right path, I needed to make up with Dev. Despite everything that had happened at the club and everything that was surely to happen Monday morning at school, courtesy of the Proud Crowd and their JV minions, what I cared most about repairing was my friendship with Dev. We had both taken a turn toward the dark side, seduced by the siren call of popularity. We wanted to be remembered for being more than just average, and now we would both always remember, perhaps more than anything else, how we destroyed our senior spring and possibly our friendship. We were both guilty, I knew that much, but I also knew that we had both been driven blind by the Market.

I snuck downstairs, trying not to stir my parents. I could hear the late Sunday football game in the living room and Dad's snoring. A perfect cover for a late-night departure. I tiptoed into the family room and then through the mudroom door, and slipped out into the night. It was nearly summer, but the air still had a cool bite, and I took a big gulp of air and felt my lungs expand. With each breath I took, a bit of hope filled me, and like a newborn free from its mother for the first time, I couldn't take in enough oxygen. A torrent of emotion welled up inside, but I pushed it down.

I'm not going to cry anymore, I told myself.

When I pulled on the door handle of my car, I discovered it was locked, so I reached into my purse and fished around for my keys. That's when I heard the front door open and saw my mom step outside. I searched her face to see what emotion it held—anger, sorrow, disappointment—but the porch light created a halo around her head and obscured her expression. I turned and faced her head-on. I was ready to tell her everything. To tell her how her daughter had sunk to new lows just to be popular. How her daughter had really just mimicked her mother's own desires to be "in the club."

"Need these?" she said, dangling the keys.

I could see her eyes now. They were sad and the moon shadow made them only sadder.

"I do."

"I heard about what happened last night. All of it."

Yeah. I wager the whole town had.

I said nothing, awaiting my certain death sentence. Would it be by firing squad or lethal injection?

"How did you get home?" she asked.

Not the next question I was expecting.

"I walked, part of the way. Jack Clayton from the bookstore drove me the rest of the way."

"Mrs. Sawyer called me last night," she said simply. "She told me . . . what you've been going through. I didn't realize."

"I was a fool."

She didn't say anything. She just walked up to me and put her arms around me and let me have a long hug. My chest heaved a few times, but I didn't let a tear fall. I could hear her sniffle, and her voice kept catching as she tried to speak. Even in the thick swirl of emotion, I knew I'd never forget this moment. I gripped her hard for another few seconds and then released.

"Sorry," I said. The word tumbled from my lips unexpectedly, without an ounce of reluctance. For years, since middle school, perhaps, we had been sparring with each other over every inch of territory. But tonight we each ceded some ground for what I knew would be a new friendship. It felt good, natural, like it was something that had always been on the horizon but we were just unable to see it.

"Me, too," she said.

"About the club, I'm sorry. I guess I really screwed it up for you."

She played with my hair and shook her head.

"I wouldn't want to be somewhere with people who'd treat my daughter like that." After a moment, she laughed a little. "Besides, I think your dad is happy."

She handed me the keys, and I smiled. "I guess so."

"Let me know how late you'll be, so I don't worry?"

I nodded.

That much I could certainly do.

I took the long way over to Dev's house. I needed time to sort out what I was going to say to her. Somehow, the simple "sorry" my mom and I had made up with a few minutes earlier wouldn't be nearly enough. I thought about telling her why we should never have started with the Market, of explaining how her obsession with my popularity drove me bananas, of asking her how long she knew Gretchen and Will had been conspiring against me, but I knew she'd have her own tale to tell. How I had forgotten our pact to expose and take down the Market, how I had forgotten about her and Callie in my quest to become popular and be part of the Proud Crowd, and it would all be true, sadly. We were guilty of abusing our friendship, and I wasn't sure how to get it back.

I pulled up to the curb in front of her house and watched as a young family arrived home across the street, the father hoisting his little girl up onto his shoulders. I sat in my car for a few minutes and thought about being a child and that innocent period when you're unaware of anything outside of your own little world. Not wealth, not boys, not popularity.

After a few moments, I pulled out my phone and hit Dev's number on my speed dial. She picked up on the third ring.

"Yeah," she said. Her voice had a coldness I had never encountered before, and it struck me that it was pretty much how hate sounded.

"Come down. I'm out front."

There was a click and the line went dead. She drew the curtains back in her room, a triangle of light framing her small form, and then she let them go. For a few moments I worried she might not come, but then her front porch light went off and the door opened. I guess she didn't want her parents to see us.

When she got in the car—the hood on her gray sweatshirt pulled up—she stared out the windshield, refusing to look at me. I did the same, unwilling to yield the high ground. If I did, I knew we'd never be friends again. We needed to understand that what happened was a team effort, that we had brought this plight upon ourselves.

"What do your parents know?" I asked.

"Nothing," she said. "Except what your mom told my mom. They spoke last night."

"Good, that's good," I said. "So I guess you know what happened last night?"

A little grin caught her by surprise, but she quickly suppressed it.

"I'm sorry, Dev."

"Me too," she said. "But I can't even look at you right now. I can't think about you."

"We let ourselves get carried away. It wasn't me or you talking yesterday. Whoever we were disappeared a few weeks ago."

She nodded, and tears filled her eyes and then poured down her cheeks. I held mine in place, though inside I was drowning.

"I don't trust you anymore," she said, and I felt myself pull back in surprise. "I could never trust you again."

"Why? Because I took our dream too far? And you didn't?"

"You bit the apple . . ."

I was trying to process what she was saying. It was true, I suppose; I had tasted the popular life, and truth be told, I didn't want to go back. I couldn't, I guess. No matter what happened tomorrow at school—and total social pariah was the most likely outcome—I'd never go back to being the old Katie Winthrop. That was the price I'd pay for flying too high.

But did that mean we couldn't be friends anymore?

"You're being dramatic, Dev. It's not like I passed through a door that can't be opened again."

"It is, actually," she said. Her voice was tiny, mouselike. "It is. You made me feel unworthy of you. Your eyes, these past few weeks, told me I wasn't good enough. I can't look at you now and think that isn't what you still believe."

"C'mon, Dev."

Without a word, Dev opened the door and stepped out. She shut the door quietly, as if she were being careful not to break something, and shuffled her way back toward her house. On her front steps, she glanced over at me one last time; but just when I thought she might say something, she shook her head and disappeared into her house, and the lights in the foyer clicked off.

CHAPTER

28

THE MONDAY FOLLOWING the Black & White fiasco was supposed to be the beginning of the most fun and memorable week of any we had had as a class. Senior Week at Millbank High was a euphemism for doing absolutely nothing. Sure, it was anything but a party for the juniors, who were taking finals and desperately hoping to improve their GPAs before applying to colleges that fall, but for the seniors, the week translated to day after day of no classes, no worries, and a whole lot of letting loose, both in and out of school.

That morning, however, I was surely the only senior at MHS who was dreading the week. As I drove up North Adams toward my parking spot for the last year, I braced myself for what lay ahead, and it definitely wasn't going to be pretty. Slyly working your way up the Market was one thing. Leading a crazy one-person public attack on the most popular girl in school . . . well, that was something else altogether.

The festivities began as soon as I set foot in school. Walking down the hallway toward my locker, I could feel people looking at me askance—suspicious, smirking—and behind me as I passed, I could hear whispers and giggles. Like some death-row inmate taking that final trip toward the chair, with all her fellow prisoners eyeing her as she passed, I walked, eyes focused on the floor, hoping just to make it to my locker without breaking down. *Dead girl walking.*

When I got to my locker, I got my first taste of what was sure to come. The door had been keyed. *140* had been permanently etched into the cheap green paint.

I knew what it meant, of course, but a month ago, when I agonized about being labeled Seventy-one, I had completely ignored the fact that there was a Seventy-two, and Seventy-three, and worse, a One hundred forty. How was it that I could agonize so deeply about my own plight, but fail to imagine the utter pain of being One hundred forty? But then here was a stranger thing—I couldn't even remember who One hundred forty was. Wasn't that the ultimate irony of the Market? It was a ranking of everyone, but all we (or maybe I) thought of was ourselves.

I opened my locker to find ten or twelve invitations for Heaven laying haphazardly on the bottom. People had slid them through the small vents on the top of my locker. I opened the top one and written in red lipstick were the words, "Die Bitch."

Look, ma, I'm on top of the world.

I picked the others off the floor and stuffed them into my book bag. There was no point in reading them—I was sure they all said the same thing. I closed my locker, leaned on the cold metal, and took a deep breath. I knew the moment I sat down in my homeroom seat, the real chaos would begin. Now that I was no longer a moving target, someone was bound to get the courage to actually ask me what happened Saturday night, and I really didn't know what I was going to say—I mean, I couldn't tell them the truth, about the Market, about Gretchen and Will, about how messed up the world of MHS had become, about how crazed I myself had become in effort to be considered "good enough" for some invisible group of tastemakers, about—

"Ms. Winthrop?" said a deep voice from behind me. I turned and looked up into the eyes of Francis Johnson, the principal of MHS.

"Yes?"

"Come with me."

We walked toward his office in what felt like superslow motion. If all eyes were on me before, it's hard to describe the heaviness of the attention I was now receiving. Teachers, administrators, rent-a-cops, students from every class—they all watched as Principal Johnson escorted me down the hall.

When we reached the waiting room outside his office, he turned.

"Sit. Wait. Don't speak until I come for you."

I gulped and nodded. There were two couches, and one was filled with boxes and files. I felt rattled and I looked down at my hands; they were shaking like I'd had twenty espressos at Starbucks before coming to school. I clasped them together in an effort to look cool under pressure. Never having been to the principal's office in my entire career, except to pick up the certificate for being a National Merit Scholar—ah, how far I'd fallen—I was scared to death. Was he going to call my parents? Would he suspend me from graduation?

I could feel my heart racing and my ears ringing from the rise in my blood pressure. Then Vice Principal Taylor, as if on cue, delivered his version of a massive sedative: he marched Gretchen Tanner in and seated her right beside me. My heart screeched to a halt, and my nerves suddenly went steely. If Johnson was going to drag us both in, I wasn't going to hold back. I'd take her, her crew, and the damn Market down for good. Gretchen stared directly at the wall and made no sign of actually acknowledging that I was sitting next to her. As always, her skin was beautiful, but beneath the makeup, I could see dark rings under her eyes. She probably hadn't slept since Saturday.

"Ms. Winthrop," said Principal Johnson. "Come in."

I stood up and walked by Gretchen, and for the first time that morning, our eyes met in an intimate way. She was trying to say something, but what, I had no idea. A plea for mercy, perhaps? Well, as I walked into Principal Johnson's office, I didn't feel an ounce of guilt for what I was about to do. If I was going to get busted for what happened at the Black & White, then Gretchen was going down with me. I'd tell them everything.

It was the usual school executive's office—small bookshelf of teaching-and-administrative philosophy books, a few framed degrees, and a large oak-veneer desk cluttered with papers and family photos. Nothing fancy, but enough stuff to let you know he wasn't just a teacher. No doubt the politics of MHS on the teacher and administrator level suffered from its own version of "Us and Them."

Johnson sat heavily in a large, black leather swivel chair. He was a big man with dark-brown skin and a bushy black beard salted with white whiskers.

"Do you know why you're here?" he asked.

I did know why I was there, and though I'd never been in this kind of situation before, I knew enough from watching *Law & Order* not to give any information unless I was physically compelled to do so. I needed to see exactly what his agenda was.

"No," I answered innocently. "Not really."

"Do you think you can stonewall me, Ms. Winthrop?"

He was leaning over his desk now, and I could smell the stale coffee on his breath.

"Why don't you tell me why you and Gretchen had an altercation at the Black & White?"

"That's not a school event—why do you care?"

His eyes flared. He was sending a message via his mind: *Don't test me or I'll squash you.* How many times had a scared student come into these offices and been crushed under his power? He'd probably imagined that since I'd been such a Goody Two-shoes, I'd kowtow in a matter of seconds.

I guess he missed the memo that things had changed.

"There's more to this and we know it," he pushed.

"I'm not sure what you are talking about, sir."

He sat back and eyeballed me for a moment. Above us, the fluorescent lights hummed.

Spinning his chair around to a stack of files behind his desk, he picked up the lone red one from the pile. It had a white sticker on its tab section, and even from where I was sitting I could read the label: THE MARKET. He opened it up, pulled out a sheet of paper, and slid it across the desk so I could read it. It was a printout from the Market—the rankings as of May 24th.

They'd known about it all along?

"Why are you showing me this?"

"Surely you don't expect me to believe you've never seen this before?"

"No," I said. "I've seen it, but I had nothing to do with it."

What else was there to say, but the truth?

"Kate, I know how far you've come, so to speak."

How far I had come? Had he tracked my climb? Did he know that I went from Seventy-one to Blue Chip? Did he know about me and Dev? About my little fake tragedy? Did he know about Will and Gretchen and their plan to use me in their little stock scam? These questions, and many more, rocketed through my head, and I struggled to see where this was all leading.

"I'm not sure I follow," I said.

"We've been aware of the Market for a month or so now. We haven't closed it down for two reasons. First, it appears to have been accessible to only a very small group of students; and second, because we wanted to catch those who were behind it. I know, for whatever reason, you were somebody who caught the eye of the Market and became a success."

"Look, I don't know who was running the Market, and I don't know why they were interested in me."

He put his hands on his face and rubbed his eyes, and then he crossed them like a little boy might when about to begin prayer.

"Let's start over. We're fairly certain Gretchen Tanner was involved. It appears some group bet a lot of money on you, and your unlikely rise to the top certainly assured them of winning. So here's what I think: Gretchen, and whoever else, used you, Kate. You found out about it, and you took out your anger on Gretchen at the Black & White. Is that right?"

I sat still and didn't allow a single muscle to twitch. I didn't blink or scratch my wrist or rub my eyes. This was it—my chance to annihilate Gretchen, Will, and everyone else who'd wronged me in last few weeks.

"Care to elaborate?" He smiled. "We can make this all go away for you."

I won't lie: the words "used you" made my stomach twist in knots, and I wanted revenge. To rain destruction like hellfire down on that smug, confident little world that was inhabited by Gretchen Tanner and every other girl like her. And I was about to tell him everything I knew . . . the whole story from the very beginning . . . but something stopped me.

I thought of Mrs. Sawyer and how she questioned me the last time I'd seen her. And I kept coming back to my deepest feelings, which all revolved around one true fact: I'd wanted what they—what the Market—had to offer. If I'd been truly offended by the Market, even from the get-go, I would've walked away from the whole thing. Sure, I knew it was a kind of fantasy, that whatever the Market said was only one subjective view on "popularity," but it was a fantasy of which I wanted to be part. No one had forced me into it.

"There's no one to take down," I answered after a period of silence. "It's like the real world, Mr. Johnson. Nobody, not even Gretchen, creates popularity—it's just there. None of us knew who created the Market. We were just players, in one way or another."

Now it was his turn to be silent. He sat leaning back in his chair, the support creaking under his girth.

"The Market is dead—just leave it that way," I whispered. "We'd all be better off."

"I can't do that now. This was illegal gambling. Besides, your escapades on Saturday upset a lot of people, important people."

"Club people, you mean?" He didn't respond. "Are they your Proud Crowd, Mr. Johnson?"

"Watch it, young lady," he said. "This isn't going to die."

"No, you're right about that, but that's for next year's class to handle. For me, it died two days ago."

Just then his phone rang, and the secretary announced that the superintendent was on the line. Without excusing himself, he took the call, swiveling his chair around so he was staring out the window with his back was to me. He mumbled so softly that I couldn't make out what he was saying, but I knew it was about me and Gretchen.

A thought sprang into my mind, and I reached into my book bag and tore out a piece of paper. I quickly wrote the following note:

> Gretchen,
> I didn't say anything. Don't give yourself up no matter what he says to scare you. He knows nothing.
> K

Mr. Johnson hung up, and I quickly folded the note before he turned back to me.

"That was the superintendent. He's recommending suspension during Senior Week for you and Ms. Tanner. You'll be allowed to graduate, but will not be able to participate in any other activities planned by the school . . . unless you have something to share?"

It's called "hardball" because when it hits you, it hurts. I was mute for a moment, before choosing my course.

"I'll tell you what concerns *me*," I began.

He leaned forward with a pleased smile on his face.

"I'm concerned that you were aware of the Market and let it go on for so long. Some of us could have been deeply scarred over the past month. I think my parents would be concerned about that, too."

His eyes widened, and I could tell I had his attention. The words "law" and "suit" no doubt passed through his mind.

"I'm going to go now," I said as I rose. "As I said, I consider the Market a dead issue, and I couldn't care less about Senior Week and anything else related to this school. Call my parents if you want to. I suspect they will care—but in a way you wouldn't like."

I turned and walked out the door. I expected to hear him scream my name or for him to physically stop me, but my not-so-veiled threat must have left him tongue-tied.

From the couch, Gretchen looked up as I approached, and I could tell she had been crying.

"Hey," I said, and without missing a step, I thrust the note I'd written into her hand.

I had no idea if she was going to read it, but at that moment, I felt like I had finally found peace with everything that had happened.

Gretchen Tanner was not a good person, but she was part of the hundred and forty senior girls of Millbank just the same. Sure, I could've taken her down, but what good would that have done? I would have delivered some sad little comeuppance, courtesy of the principal's office, which in the end would just have been another example of a girl taking down a girl at the request of a man—albeit the principal. And wasn't that where all this began? When I allowed myself to be judged against another girl? Did I truly believe I was any better a person than Gretchen Tanner? In my heart, I wanted to believe I was; but knowing my sins, was I worthy of being her judge and jury? Had I grown up in her house, with her mother, her money, and her beauty, would I have come out any differently than she did?

I hoped I would've, but at that moment, after spending a month realizing how weak I could be, I wasn't sure. I just knew that I hadn't earned the right to sit in judgment of her, or anybody else.

CHAPTER

29

I WALKED OUT of MHS that day knowing I'd never again pass through those doors. Whatever fond memories I may have had prior to the Market had now disappeared like the Web site itself.

The next few days were a blur of depression. I left Dev several messages, hoping we could bring things back to normal, but I only got her voice mail and never a call back. Callie and I spoke once, but she was so busy with graduation (she was on the graduation committee—and needless to say, she wanted everyone, especially herself, to look just right), she didn't have time to see me.

The day before graduation, the only place I had to be was the BookStop. When I got there, I learned that Mrs. Sawyer, who was on vacation to see her sister in North

Carolina, had left a little graduation gift for me. No surprise here—it was a book. But she had taken the time to wrap it up and put a nice pink ribbon on it, and I took it to the back room so I could open it alone. I tore open the paper, and beneath I could see the worn cover of a used book: *The Wings of the Dove* by Henry James. I hadn't read any James, aside from the scrap excerpt here and there in class, and as I flipped through it I found a letter tucked inside the flap.

Dear Kate,

I'm so proud to know you. This is one of those stories James liked to write, about a girl named Millie, an American innocent. She falls prey to two Londoners who scheme to steal her fortune by wooing her heart. She teaches them something, though, about love and its power—for both good and bad. It is one of my favorites, and this is a first edition. Treasure it as I have treasured knowing you.

Always your friend,
B.

A tear came to my eye. I always knew that Mrs. Sawyer had had a soft spot for me, but I now realized how much I meant to her. I carefully turned the book over a few times and gently placed it in my bag. At least my relationship with Mrs. Sawyer had survived the Market. It was a small consolation, but the thought that I did have a true friend out there, somewhere, made me smile. She may have been fifty-eight years my elder, but she was my friend. And now, more than ever, I realized how dear true friends were, and how painful they were to lose.

Time flew by that day at the BookStop. With Mrs. Sawyer out, Howie ran the show. He was a little more hands-on and he liked to have all the books shelved at the end of each day, so there was never any downtime whatsoever, even between seven and nine p.m. when normally the store emptied out. At eight thirty p.m., I was manning the register and it looked like I might get out before closing, but then Hal Allen came in with four boxes of books to trade in for store credit. Normally, we ask people who are selling books to make an appointment, but Mr. Allen was an old friend of the store, and we did so much business with him (I think he worked in publishing) that Howie felt obligated.

As Howie reviewed each book, he placed them on different carts: one for the first floor (recently published fiction and nonfiction), one for the second (hardcover nonfiction), and one for the basement (paperbacks). I knew Howie wouldn't let me leave until all of Allen's new arrivals were shelved, so I grabbed the paperback cart as soon as Howie finished filling it up. I rode the freight elevator down and exited with the cart into the basement stacks. The first thing I did was alphabetize the books, which took a good fifteen minutes, and then I started to shelve. The cart was overloaded, so I knew I wouldn't be home until ten. Not that it mattered much—I had no friends and no plans.

At nine fifteen, Howie called down on the interoffice phone and said he was closing at nine thirty, to finish what I had on my cart, and he would handle the rest in the morning. I took the last fifteen paperbacks and carried them by hand to the "Romance" room, where we kept all of our novels for women of a certain age (apparently Mr. Allen's wife liked bodice rippers). Men like Fabio always graced the cover with shirts torn off and muscles flexing, and women fell faint in their presence. I quickly began stacking the books, but it was hard work because the shelves were overflowing, so in an effort to make room, I started plucking duplicate titles and making a stack of them that I'd bring to Howie for storage. As I rearranged the shelf, I became lost in my own thoughts about tomorrow. I couldn't believe it was graduation day. No more high school. No more Millbank. Tomorrow was going to be first day of the rest of my life, I told myself. It wouldn't be what I expected, but I was excited, nonetheless, to move on.

I heard the elevator kick into gear, and I took the last duplicate novel off the top shelf and walked back to the elevator to meet Howie. When the doors opened, my heart skipped a beat. There, standing before me, was Will B. His hair was its usual faux-messy style and he had two or three days' worth of stubble. A week ago, I would have been swooning, but tonight the sight of his face made me feel sick. As beautiful as it was, I could see nothing but the ugliness underneath.

"Hey," he said.

"Hey."

There was a long awkward pause.

"What are you reading?" he said finally, pointing to the book in my hand.

I looked at the book. It was *Eternity* by Daphne Dugan.

"Trash," I said. "I'm just shelving trash."

We stood there awkwardly, not knowing what to say to each other.

"I came by because I wanted to tell you something."

"More lies?" I snapped. "What do you want?"

He stared at me, and I think he whispered "You," or at least that's how I read his lips.

"Don't say 'me,' Will! Don't say 'me'!"

"I fell in love with you," he said. "I love you."

"Everything about you is a fraud."

He had tears in his eyes, and for a moment I felt a twinge of forgiveness flow through my veins. I wanted so badly to go back in time—to that first bloom of feelings between us, when I believed in his true feelings. But that would never happen. He was being sincere, there was no question about that, but how could I ever manage to trust him? Even as the phrase echoed in my head, I was conscious of the fact that those were the exact same words Dev had said to me a few days ago.

"I don't trust you, Will."

"You shouldn't, but let me explain."

"I'm going home, excuse me." I walked around him, hit the elevator button, and the doors slid open immediately. I stepped in, but he managed to jump in with me before the doors shut. The freight elevator was numbingly slow, and the sound of the old-fashioned motor made it difficult to have a conversation.

"Listen," he shouted. "What happened was out of control, but I did fall in love with you, and you fell in love with me . . . didn't you?"

I didn't have to think about that answer very long because I knew the answer was "yes."

"What difference does that make? I can never look at you again without thinking you used me to play some stupid game."

"I tried to tell you several times but I didn't know how, and then it snowballed and I thought, or maybe just naively hoped, it might all just blow over once we graduated. And you'd never know."

"But I do know, and 'we' will never be again." I stepped off the elevator and strode as quickly as I could toward the front door. Howie was standing there with his keys in the door, waiting to let me out.

"Everything all right?" he asked, casting a glance at Will.

"Nothing I can't handle," I answered.

He smiled like he knew that firsthand.

I walked out into the night air. It was warm and sweet, the way only an early summer night can be. Will followed me all the way out to my car.

"So there's nothing, then?" he said.

"No, there's nothing left."

We stood there staring at each other, and my heart was exploding beneath my chest, but I held back the tears. I would not cry for this boy ever again, I told myself.

"That night when you approached me at Gretchen's party—did you know then?"

He kicked the tire of my car gently and looked up to the sky and into the stars, searching for the right words.

"Jack had a thing for you. He'd been going on about you for weeks; about how great he thought you were—"

"Did you know?"

He sighed. "Yes."

"So you're the one who put the invitation in my locker?"

"I'd put five hundred dollars in the Market and I was in last place. I'd made stupid picks and I was screwed," he began. "I told Gretchen, and she offered to stake me more money if we played together. She said she'd help me make it back—and more."

"Why didn't she just invest herself?"

"She thought it would be a fun project—for 'us,'" he said as the edge of his lip curled. "You read between the lines."

Of course.

"I was just supposed to take you on a few dates. Make people notice you," he continued. "I didn't realize how right Jack was—that I'd fall for you so hard—until it was too late."

"How could you do that to me? To Jack?"

"I couldn't turn her down! I was desperate," he said, wild-eyed. "I needed to win—for the money!"

"Is that your pathetic excuse? Money?"

"You don't understand what it's like . . . hanging around Gretchen . . . the guys," he said as he looked off into the distance. "When you're around people with so much money all the time, you realize how little you have. With her I saw what it was like. And I just . . . I wanted to be like them. Me, but better."

I suddenly saw Will for who he was—someone who had once been good, but who over time had been corrupted, not by Gretchen, but by the promise of a life that wasn't his. Gazing at him, I saw he was being torn apart, the person who he truly was battling with an image of what he so desperately wanted to be. I thought then of the afternoon I'd met his father and realized that Will hated him because he reminded Will of who he actually was: not one of the Proud Crowd.

"Why would you need any of that?" I said quietly. "It's sad."

"What about you?" he whispered. "What about your plan to climb the Market? You and Dev. I have eyes, too, you know."

How did he know about Dev and me? Who could have told him? But he didn't wait for me to respond, and instead he turned around and started walking up River Road. I stood there watching his dark jacket and jeans disappear into the night. After a few moments, I could only see his shadow, and then nothing. Just like that, the boy of my dreams had come into my life, stirred passion in my heart, and now he had disappeared, like a faint memory.

I realized then that after four years with the same group of people, there are no secrets. My sins were his sins and his sins were my own. Yes, I believed his were the worse of the two, but mine no less tragic.

As I slid into my car, I was still holding *Eternity*. I looked at the cover again, at the man with the long flowing hair and ripped muscles, battling a tiger on top of a hill, and I wondered if the last woman who read this believed in him as deeply as I had believed in my own Prince Charming.

CHAPTER

30

HIGH SCHOOL was officially over.

When Principal Johnson handed me my diploma, he was gracious and politic. He guided me in close to him and whispered, "I'm sorry it ended the way it did—you were a model student and you'll be missed." Then, as with every other student who now clutched that piece of paper in their hand, he turned toward the photographer just offstage, who was there to commemorate the occasion. We both gave thousand-watt smiles, and if some student fifty years from now were to stumble upon that photograph in a dusty old yearbook, he or she would never know what lay beneath the surface.

I exited the stage, took in my class one last time, and a few moments later we all tossed our caps high, high into the air. Callie and I found each other in the crowd and hugged, and Dev and I managed cordial nods. By noon, families headed from Lafayette Park and made their way to afternoon parties. My parents invited our extended family over— aunts, uncles, cousins, etc.—and all in all, it was about thirty people. They stayed for a few hours, congratulating me on my success, asking about my future plans. As dusk settled in, they all departed, and I found myself standing alone in our garden.

I'd warned my mom that the party Gretchen and I had planned was off. After the Black & White, I knew nobody would come, especially if Gretchen decided it wasn't the thing to do. No doubt she'd organized her own bash and had drawn most of the senior class. I'm sure I could have coaxed a few stragglers in, but why? I didn't want a room full of strangers, and truthfully, I wasn't in the mood for a celebration anyway. What I really wanted was to spend the night with Callie and Dev. Callie promised to swing by at some point that night, but she couldn't commit to a time because her mom's family was in from out of state, and nothing had changed on the Dev front, so it looked like I was going to be spending the night on my own.

My parents had made plans to go into the city. When planning the party, I'd told them they had to be nowhere in sight, so Dad had surprised Mom with tickets to a Broadway show and a meal at the Palm afterward. Now that the party wasn't happening, they asked if I wanted to come, a pity move that I actually appreciated but declined, and they were off.

I shut the lights off around most of the house, lay down in bed, and took out the book Mrs. Sawyer had given me. The pages were old and brittle, and I was careful to turn them gently. I didn't get very far into the novel when the doorbell rang. I blew out the candle I'd lit by my bed and went downstairs. I took a peek out the window beside the front door before opening it, and there, standing stiffly, was Jack Clayton.

"Jack," I said. "Come in."

He looked around as he stepped into our foyer. "I'm the first, then," he said.

"And the last," I said with a smile.

"What's that?" he said. "Isn't there a party tonight?"

"No," I said. "I mean, Gretchen's throwing something, I think, but not here. I just assumed you'd be there, with everyone else."

He neither smiled nor frowned. He just mumbled something to himself and handed me his coat. Then he brandished a six-pack of beer and gave me his keys. "Hold these for me and don't let me leave plastered."

"Jack—there's no party. I mean, you can stay, but it would just be me and you."

"Sounds like a party to me," he quipped.

We both stood there for a moment—the truth of how I'd treated him between us.

"You don't have to stay, just because you came by mistake," I offered. "I know I let you down. I know how I screwed things up."

"You did."

"So why are you staying?" I asked meekly.

"Let's just say I'm big on second chances." He popped off a bottle cap. A beat later, he opened another and handed me a bottle. We tapped glass and took a big swallow of beer. I smiled at him for what felt like a full minute.

"What's so funny?"

"Nothing—I'm happy you're here, with me," I said. "Thank you."

I moved toward him and gave him a big hug. Nothing romantic, mind you, but a hug for being there. It was true that he was a recent friend, but I was thinking Dev needed to add a new theory to her Latebloomer model. The Latebloomer friend: it's a phenomenon that often occurs late in senior year when silly social guards are dropped, and a friendship that had been heretofore impossible to imagine blooms in the spring sun.

As we broke from our embrace, I couldn't help but think back to that night in Dickey Dogs when we kissed, and for a moment, I felt real passion. I knew now that I'd missed a chance with him. Happiness? True love? A one-month fling? I'd never know. But he had told me he liked me for me—for my natural self—and I took that sincere declaration for granted. Not for Kat or for the timid Katie. What he liked, I now realized, was the person I had mistakenly run from in my climb to the top of the Market. Simply put, he liked Kate.

I popped a bowl of popcorn, and we sat in my living room, drinking our brew and yucking it up about the BookStop. I told him about the gift Mrs. Sawyer had given me, and he looked over the volume. His hands caressed the cover, and when he opened the pages, he tenderly turned them over, careful not to fold any of the edges.

"It's beautiful, Kate."

I nodded.

By the time we got to our second beer, I was starting to feel the weight of the past week lift off my shoulders. We talked about the conversation Will and I had, and he told me that the two of them had had a throwdown as well. "We haven't spoken since," he said.

"I'm sorry, Jack."

"Don't be. We've been through a lot. We'll find a way back." He grabbed a handful of popcorn and sat back on the couch, looking up at the ceiling. The sadness of the situation enveloped the room, and I had no words to comfort him.

"Can I ask you one last thing, and then we don't ever have to talk about it again?"

He nodded.

"Did you ever invest in the Market?"

He said nothing for a moment, then smiled. "What do you think?"

I looked down at the floor sheepishly. Of course he hadn't.

A few minutes later, bizarrely, the doorbell rang again—no doubt a straggler who had heard a rumor I was throwing a party. I pulled the curtain back for the second time tonight, and the air jumped out of my lungs. Dev was standing on my stoop holding a six-pack of beer! I threw the door open and then wrapped my arms around her in uncontrollable joy.

"Don't squeeze too hard—the package is still fragile."

I stepped back and looked at her with a big smile on my face. No other person could have made me feel happier than Dev had just made me feel right then. She reached into her bag and pulled out my old jean jacket and handed it to me. I held it up, and a big smile crossed my face.

"Old blue," I said. "I missed you."

"I missed you in it," she said. "I mean, don't misunderstand me—you look a lot cuter now, but I liked the girl in the jean jacket a little bit better."

"Me too," I said. She laughed and then held out a copy of our business plan. "I want you to burn this tonight in honor of our friendship."

"I'm sorry," I said again. She looked at me and mouthed, "Me too," and then we hugged again, but for longer and with more meaning and less youthful exuberance.

From out of the darkness I heard a voice as familiar as my own, "Now that's the kind of loving I expect from the two of you."

It was Callie, and after she stepped up onto the porch, grinning from ear to ear, we circle-hugged like the high school girls we were. It was all like a dream, like the past month had never happened, though we all knew it had. We probably would never trust again, at least not in the naive way that we had, but perhaps we'd created a new level of trust, one earned rather than assumed. We all knew what it meant to have such great friends, and never again would I take that for granted.

After a few minutes of chitchat, we all moved to the back porch, and Jack entertained us with stories about playing music in dive bars and summer tours with Jane Austen's Secret Lover. Callie and Dev knew Jack, but they had never really spoken to him, and I could tell that Dev took an immediate shine to him, and he to her. And Callie, well it wasn't hard for any guy to fall under her spell.

It was about a half hour later that a stream of headlights started pouring down Woodside, my block. Dev noticed them first, and I looked out toward the street, bewildered. One by one the cars rumbled down my street and parked. In each car, two and sometimes four students from our class piled out, one after another. Jack stood up, walked through the house, and opened the front door. Within fifteen minutes, a waterfall of students fell in and moved out to my backyard. Paul Skibnewski and Kevin Healy from the football team lumbered out, kegs on their shoulders, and a very conscientious girl from the graduation committee collected keys from all the drivers. Warren Rabin pulled his SUV up to the end of the driveway, opened his lift gate—exposing huge speakers—and turned on the music. Within a matter of minutes, my quiet night with friends transformed itself into a rager with my entire senior class. It was surreal, I admit, but I couldn't help but smile.

As I looked around, I could scarcely keep count of the numbers. It was an eclectic mix ranging from the Proud Crowd, to the Goth kids, to the president of the Latin Club (who had stunned everyone by winning the schoolwide talent show, singing a Stevie Wonder song with a karaoke machine). In my twelve years in the Millbank school system, I had never once witnessed such a coming together. Had the euphoria of actually earning our degrees exploded all the imaginary social barriers we had placed between ourselves and our fellow classmates?

From the corner of my eye, I recognized the listless saunter of Will, entering the outer edges of the party. Frankly, I didn't know how to react, and I braced for an unpleasant scene when I saw Jack walk up to Will. For a few moments they stood there toe-to-toe, exchanging some words. Jack, who was a few inches taller than Will, opened his arms and embraced him in a man-hug. Then Jack turned in my direction and pointed, and I saw Will make his way through the crowd and up the stairs toward me. It gave me time to prepare, but nothing came to mind. What more was there to say than what we had said last night?

When Will reached the top step, he stood there until I gave him a nod that it was okay for him to approach. He hopped up and walked over to me, but not too close.

"I'm not staying," he said. "But I couldn't let this day pass without saying something: you were the best thing that happened to me."

"Are those *your* words?" I said. It was a smart-ass thing to say, but my heart was still raw.

"They all are now," he said with a weird little grin. "This is me."

"Okay," I said. "Thanks."

I didn't feel the same way. In fact, I pretty much felt the opposite, but by now we were past recriminations. We said nothing, and Will looked down at the gray planks of the deck.

"You should stay," I said, staring out into the sea of seniors occupying my backyard. "This isn't about us—it's bigger than us."

Then he said something I didn't expect at all.

"Gretchen did this."

My head snapped around and I stared at him hard. He didn't turn my way, but he knew I was looking at him.

"That was real . . . what you did for her the other day. The note, I wouldn't have done it."

"She told you?"

He nodded and then took a pull off his beer. "She told everyone that they should come here."

She did that? Really?

"Is she here?"

"Yeah. On your stoop chatting with a few friends."

Weaving between party-goers, I walked toward the sliding glass door off the deck. It was already open, and I pushed the curtains over, before looking back at Will. His eyes were still on me.

"You're staying," I called.

He nodded and walked over to me and put his arms around me. I embraced him. A little sob slipped and my chest shuddered, but I caught myself. He whispered something to me that I couldn't quite make out, but it didn't matter. We'd never be together again, and all his apologies would never mend my heart enough to trust him. But I suppose the sincerity in his voice, not the words themselves, felt honest and truthful.

I let go, and he disappeared behind the drapes. I walked

slowly to the front of the house and opened the door. Sure enough, Gretchen was sitting there on my stoop. We had come full circle from six weeks ago when I was stranded on *her* stoop, trying to figure out how I was going to get home. She looked up, and her little entourage—Jodi, Elisa, Carrie—all looked up, too.

"Can we talk?" I asked.

Gretchen chinned her posse away, and they stood up and walked around the side of the house. We waited a few moments to make sure we were alone.

"I'll leave," she said. "I just wanted to make sure everything was under control."

"Why did you do this?" I said, waving to the back of the house.

"Why did you give me that note?" she countered. I wasn't ready for that sharp of a response, but I guess I shouldn't have been surprised. We had ripped each other apart over the past week and there was no reason to hide behind niceties.

"I was tired," I said, taking a deep breath. "Just tired."

There was so much more to it, of course—I was tired of being at war, with Gretchen, with what people expected, believed, imagined—but sometimes things are best left unspoken.

"Yeah, me too," she said. A few moments of silence passed, and then she added, "It won't make you feel better, but it was innocent. It was a game, and then it became real."

"It was always real," I said. "It just made us feel better to pretend it was a game."

That was the thing I learned after four years. Popularity is *both* imagined and real. It's in my head as much as it's in Gretchen's or Dev's. But outside of us, outside the understanding of any one person, it existed as a very real thing. The Market, its valuations, were ridiculous and meaningless. Simply put, it represented the musings of a handful of kids who got their jollies judging others. But for those of us drawn into its world, it was as real and painful as anything could be.

Gretchen's eyes flickered. "No more games," she said with more sincerity than I believed she was capable of mustering.

"You can't say that and mean it forever," I said. "But I guess we can say it to each other. No more games between *us*."

"Between us," she echoed. "Yes. I meant just between us."

We sat there for a few minutes longer, looking into the night, not speaking. The stars twinkled like faraway stage lights. In the background, I could hear hundreds of voices colliding behind us, melting into one loud roar of relief.